Kismet's A Witch

Jaelle Keyes

Acknowledgments

Linda and team from Linda Edits- grammar police, plot fixer, and all-around best editor in the world, I couldn't have done any of this without you. https://www.lindaedits.com

Julie S. from J S Designs Cover Art- thanks for the gorgeous cover, advice, and friendship. You are so talented. https://jsdesignscoverart.com

The Hangout- Vee R. Paxton, and all the rest of you – you are the best advice givers, critique partners, brainstorming helpers, and beta readers in the world. I cherish your friendships and I'm so grateful for your encouragement.

And finally, my husband Mark- you are my rock, my love, my support. Thank you for your encouragement and celebrating with me whether I've written 50 or 50,000 words.

Contents

Prologue

Nola

Other than the ticking of the cooling engine and the slamming of the screen door as Jasmine leaves the house to help carry groceries, the world around me has gone completely silent. No bees buzz around the daisies and poppies in the field. No birds flit in and out of the bushes or trees. Even the light June breeze stills. It's as if the universe is holding its breath. A collective pause, one moment, and then two before the gravel beneath my feet begins to vibrate.

There's knowing something is going to happen—I've seen this scene so many times before in my mind, that I'm torn between vision and reality—and then there's experiencing it for real. This feels different, more robust, raw, powerful.

It's odd how visions can omit some of the details, like smells and small noises, but amplify others like the taste of dust lifting into the air. Jasmine races toward me, the veil of sadness that has hung off her since her boyfriend left replaced with the dawning horror of what I warned her and the others would come has arrived.

"Nola! Is this it? Is it happening?" Her shout is echoed by Tanni's and Ginger's cries of terror from within our little Cape Cod-style home as the vibration builds in intensity to a ground-shaking rumble.

"I-I think so. Grab those bags and let's get inside." The visions showed me the location of the house where we would weather this cataclysm. It showed me the devastation and the time of year, but it never showed me a date.

"Oh God! I hate it when you're right!" Jasmine yells as we grab the last of the grocery bags from the trunk. In a stumbling run over the tremoring lawn, we reach the front step.

"Hurry!" I hate it when I'm right too. This is going to be bad. Utter annihilation.

I don't know why this little house will remain largely unaffected, but I'm trusting the vision that steered me to it to hold true. There are other places that will be spared, but most in a roughly thousand-mile radius will be wiped from existence. Vaporized.

The rumbling grows to a roar. Nearby explosions rock our little house. I cringe as I toss the groceries in a corner and follow Jasmine as she joins Tanni and Ginger under the sturdy kitchen table the two women have pushed up against the interior support wall.

A strange sucking feeling begins to pull at my body as we huddle together. I feel like a water balloon stretching as it takes its capacity of water and then some. First, a bunch of bananas and then a head of cabbage, and then other items rise from a spilled grocery bag, moving upward and out of sight above the edge of the table.

The house groans, high-pitched and chittering. I picture nails dragging across a chalkboard, but amplified a thousand times. The small hairs on the back of my neck stand up. I know we'll make it through this intact, I've seen it, but fear envelopes me anyway, making my lungs squeeze tightly in my chest.

"Please hold together...we'll be okay...please hold together...we'll be okay..." My voice restricted and wheezing from the stress. Jasmine joins my mantra, sounding just as scared as I am.

Suddenly, the table legs leave the floor along with my knees. I hold on tighter to Jasmine. She holds on to Ginger, who holds on to Tanni as we too are lifted into the air.

We're lifted high enough that I can see out the bay window in the living room. Fires burn in the distance as billowing clouds of smoke block out the light of the sun. The tabletop bangs against the ceiling, and we're pressed into the underside of the table.

The pressure is overwhelming. One of the girls cries out, Tanni, I think. It's as if a giant fist is trying to push us through the table like grapes through a sieve. Suddenly, the pressure releases, and we're slammed with the force of a speeding train back to the floor.

Chapter 1

Nola (Fifteen months later)

The sudden twitching pop of the nerve in my right eyelid is the first indication that my off-the-rails life is about to get crazier. I ignore the warning in favor of loading the two dozen salvaged cans of food into the old-fashioned baby carriage I found hanging from the ceiling in the antique shop on the other side of town.

The can labels, worn and tattered, are brittle wisps of paper, too long exposed to the elements. It'll be a surprise when we open them whether we get soup or beans. God, I pray it isn't spinach, but I've never gotten any attention from the Lord before, so I don't put much stock in beseeching someone who just doesn't give a shit. I'm more familiar with the disappointment that comes from relying on anyone else. It'd be just my luck that every single can will be filled with spinach. What's the old saying? *If it weren't for bad luck, I'd have no luck at all.*

Yeah, girls like me, with a family like mine? We don't get good luck, and I'm not even joking. Was it luck or kismet that my little white-trash mama slept with a married man at the age of sixteen, a Baptist preacher no less, and got pregnant with me? Or was it luck when he and his church ran us out of town when I started to look like him? I surely didn't feel lucky when my mama turned to alcohol and every other substance she could put in her body. It happened when boyfriend after boyfriend would leave her lying in her own disgusting filth, and I became the adult at seven years old.

The best day of my life was when my twelve-year-old self found a battered deck of tarot cards in the trash while I was digging for what mama called leftovers.

It was the best day because the cards spoke to me. I started listening to them, reading their stories and telling people's fortunes. Yup, you could say things started to look up. At least they laid down their money, and I picked it up just for telling folks what they wanted to hear.

My readings are accurate, not because of some hocus-pocus mumbo jumbo, but because each card has a story. I'm also excellent at reading people, and I tell them what they expect to hear. See, here's the thing: people already know the outcome to the questions they ask. Most just want divine or mystical confirmation. I give them that.

When I turned fourteen, I started having what I call "episodes," but if I'm truthful, most would call them visions, and not one has been wrong. *Every single one* has come to pass.

I used the information that came to me from that first episode to scare off my mama's on-again-off-again druggie boyfriend when he tried to force himself on me. I screamed at him exactly what was going to happen as I fought to get him off me, not sparing him one little detail. Furthermore, I cursed him bad in front of his friends, and he believed me. Little did he or I or anyone else know that the curse would come true a few days later.

Thereafter, my reputation grew, and most people left me alone, including mama. People still wanted to know what was in store for them, and some people wanted me to cast curses on others they thought did them wrong. I'm not proud to say it, but I did it for a price and smiled all the way to the bank with a full belly. That is, until too many of the curses became real events and I found myself on the wrong side of the law.

When my mouth grows numb, I know I'm in trouble. Instead of a trip down memory lane, I should have gotten these goods packed and hightailed it back home. I call out to Jasmine, except it comes out sounding wrong between my frozen lips. "Dazmim? Dotta doe mow."

"What did you say? Nola? What's going on?" Jasmine pokes her confused and sweaty, somewhat sad, but still gorgeous, face around the corner. The constant hot, dry breeze blows a tendril of sable colored hair into her eyes and across her cheek and lips.

"Id'z appenin' adin."

We've known each other a long time. In fact, we spent three years in juvie together. When we got out, she became a stripper and I started my tarot side hustle again, minus the curses. She's been with me through quite a few episodes and hasn't let me down yet.

"Oh shit! Let's get moving, girl!"

I'm thankful she's with me. When I started having the same three visions around four years ago, they would hit me at least once a month. In hindsight, we figured out that as the date of the first vision came closer, the frequency of these episodes came more often. Each one of them foretold a horrific and catastrophic event happening in the heartland of America. My friends and I lived through it and we're surviving in a wild and strange new world.

It's been fifteen months and eleven days since the last episode and since the apocalypse that changed everything. I tried to warn the authorities. All I got for my efforts was a psych eval and a lockup again for a seventy-two-hour observation hold.

No one would listen when I told them the world was gonna go to shit, except Jasmine and Tanni and Ginger two girls from the strip club where she worked. After Jasmine's boyfriend kicked her to the curb because of her weird friends, we pooled our resources and bought a house with a well and cistern on the outskirts of the next town over. I saw that house in the vision, and we laid in supplies for the coming cataclysm. We're glad we did too, because apart from a handful of people, there have been few survivors.

Jasmine and I hurry as fast as we can back toward the little brick house that's become our haven and the first real home any of us has ever had. It's kinda funny how the world falling apart gave each of us our first taste of the normal American dream.

I hope against hope that we make it back before we run into anyone else from this town. Not that many survived, but the ones that did, we'd rather not deal with. The second reoccurring vision is of the jerk who thinks he's in charge. For the most part, he is, for now. He has his role to play in the future, but his end isn't pretty, which leads me to the third vision of strange shape-shifting humanoid creatures with tremendous strength and otherworldly men who can wield magic. Demon or dragonesque males who throw fire and make the earth tremble. Angelic, winged beings who control lightning and wind and rain. And men with shining platinum eyes who can take on the characteristics of animals. We haven't encountered any of them yet, but I know they're coming. It's only a matter of time. I struggle with this vision the most now that the first one has come true. Is it truly a foretelling, or is it a nightmare?

By the time we get home, my fingers and toes feel like ice blocks even in the late-day heat. My gait is stilted and uneven as I drag myself up the front walk. Tanni, who's been on watch, calls out to Ginger when she sees us and helps us get the baby carriage full of goods into the house.

Jasmine takes my arm, leading me into the little bedroom we share. She helps me sit on the queen-size bed and makes quick work of removing my shoes and clothes before settling a gigantic man-sized T-shirt over my head. She helps me to lie down and then pulls a thick blanket off the shelf and settles it over me. It's just in the nick of time too, because my body begins to quake and shiver as it shuts down. My eyes roll back in my head, and I'm sucked into a new and frightening glimpse of the future that's coming for us.

Truex

The wind blows over the foothills of the mountain, cool and crisp, ruffling my black feathers as I keep watch over my prince. I give them a negligent shake, settling them back into place. The fresh scent of pine steadies the discontent that has been growing inside me ever since we were ordered to the Fae outpost of Summer's Veil.

Grief, raw and biting, rolls through me at the loss of our queen and our people in the Enlightened City. I'm one of the lucky ones. I still have my twin with me, unlike my prince. He lost our beloved Heleni, both queen and sister. Orion's stance at the edge of the plateau is stoic at first. He cocks his head, his crystalline hair lifting on the breeze for a moment before settling around his shoulders. Can he hear the cries from the past? Does he feel the same growing impotence, the same helplessness? The same gut-wrenching inertia that the loss of the Omnichronos—wild magic—our people and Atlantaes has caused?

Within the elite guard, I have always been the hothead, the grumpy asshole, the one who rushes not to just join the fight, but to start it. My brother, Tarrik, is the quiet one, stealthy and cunning, always watching, always waiting for the best opportunity to strike. That we are trapped here, immobile and without purpose, is slowly killing us, me faster than Tarrik. We have no mates and cannot have children. We have no future. Our race is doomed.

I expand my awareness, giving my senses free rein to discover any threat to my friend, my prince, the last Fae of royal blood. The straightening of Orion's posture and a wave of his hand draws my attention back to him. His demeanor is once again confident, deliberate, intense, just like it was before we left Atlantaes. It's as if he has suddenly shaken off the grief and found a new purpose. A new hope. There is something in the air. Some chimera of energy. A vibration just beyond the edge of my awareness, tickling my intuition. Anticipation bursts through my bloodstream. What is it? What does he perceive?

The crunch of snow and the brush of a pine bough announce the presence of Jahzuah, captain of the guard. Jahz is a silver-tongued worrier. His constant nagging at everyone, the prince included, used to be a great source of amusement among us. He is steadfast in his care and protection of us all. That he allowed Orion to have even this much time alone tells me he is feeling the burden of hopelessness too. His worry must be great, because he does not notice the change in Orion's demeanor as he banters and then slings his arm around him to steer him back into the fold.

My prince is up to something. Jahz does not see it. Interesting. Orion will not reveal what has changed until he is ready, and I will hold what I have observed in confidence, but the relief that washes through me lightens the weight that I carry. I drop from my perch, landing as warrior, not in the glamour of a crow. I fall into formation behind the two friends as they make their way back inside Summer's Veil, knowing that whatever Orion is up to will have a drastic effect on us all. What that something is remains to be seen, but I am more than ready.

Days later, we are planning an excursion past the Waste, the area completely wiped out by the cataclysm. We plan to visit cities that overlap with the human realm of earth to find precious stones that may fix the Omnichronos so that we may return to our home realm of Elfame.

Jahzuah is having a fit that Orion is not only traveling with us, but he will also be leading the warriors. He is champing at the bit to get moving. What does he know that the rest of us don't? Excitement bubbles up within me. We are finally again doing what Fae warriors are meant to do. Explore, fight, fuck, and adventure until our queen... My jubilation drops, sinking for a time back into the well of sorrow within me. We have no queen to direct us any longer. Therein lies the problem. We will never be what we were without a queen. The age of Fae will die with the last of us. Maybe Orion's quest to get away from Summer's Veil is only for the remembrance of better times. No mystery, no chase or pursuit.

My spirits are low until we take to the air, following our prince. Flying together as a murder of crows high over the land, protecting our prince, is the escape I need. The feel of crisp air dancing over my feathers brushes all thought away as I lose myself to the wind and sun and open land below.

Nola

The world turns to cool mist. A sheer diaphanous veil swirling and twining around me, whispering across my cheeks and temples, over my arms and fingers, encircling my torso, legs, and ankles. It's thick, yet gauzy. I worry for a moment that I might trip.

It's hollow and empty, encompassing yet intimate, quiet yet resounding, confusing in all its qualities. I'm alone. Lost as I've always been, waiting, wondering, yearning for that soul-deep connection to someone. The one I do not dwell on. The one I've almost given up on because I don't believe it exists for the likes of me.

Except...on the periphery, I can feel a presence. I've garnered something or someone's attention. The mist before me thins as glowing white snowflakes drift and fall like confetti against a blue-on-black backdrop. It's mesmerizing in its peaceful beauty.

I don't know how long I stare, but I find myself sinking deeper into the scene before me. The blue-on-black backdrop has depth, texture, and a beauty of its own. Spellbound by the flux and play of the two colors mixing, it takes me a while to realize I'm staring at feathers. Feathers of such a rich and supple black that the shimmering blue becomes the highlight, the counterpoint that saves one from sinking into nothingness.

It's those small glints of blue that bring my awareness to inquisitive eyes staring back at me. Little bits of coal, saturated with intelligence, cunning, and yes, blatant curiosity, peer at me through the mist and falling snow. It's a crow. I know that in some cultures the crow is a messenger. In others, it's a symbol of magic. Looking at the mystical bird in front of me, I understand it represents both.

The feeling of movement, of being universally connected to those keen and knowing eyes, creates a bridge of sorts, and even though I haven't taken a step, we're being maneuvered, pushed, or maybe pulled closer to each other.

The eyes begin to change from black to the same beautiful midnight cobalt on the feathers. The feathers themselves meld into hair in so many hues of shiny graphite, it could have been drawn, if drawings could be this shiny and look so fluid. The crow shifts in a glimmer of magic, a spark of light, into a male. A male who, by the first look, is all alpha, strong, and very sure of himself. His face is gorgeous, otherworldly. He isn't human. His skin is a sun-kissed honey with no wrinkles or blemishes except for the frown lines on his brow as he scowls back at me.

I have the overwhelming urge to blow him a kiss to see if his expression is frozen that way, or if his eyes will change. I'm sassy like that. Always challenging for proof, trying to be too much. Furthermore, I push to see who walks away and who will stand and fight for me. Most rarely make the effort. Blue is usually a cool color. A color of tranquility. I'm curious to know if those glittering jewels will heat with the passion of anger or, better yet, the passion between a woman and a man.

A seductive knowing gleam enters those beautiful eyes, telling me yes, they can and do change with his mood. Can he read my thoughts? An almost cruel smirk plays across his chiseled lips as he drifts on the mist toward me. When he reaches me, I tilt my head up to keep our eyes connected.

The magnetic pull I feel to him is almost hypnotic. I sway toward him until there is only a hair's breadth of distance between us. I can smell him. Sandalwood, clove, and a hint of citrus blend to create a potent mix that goes straight to my head, short-circuiting my thoughts and lighting an amorous flame deep within me. Delicious.

My hand lifts, finding a place over his heart, seemingly of its own accord. He continues to stare down into my eyes, my soul. I lick my lips, suddenly unsure. A spark of possession flashes across his face before he trails a finger over the braids resting on my chest, following them until he reaches my collarbone. The pads of his rough fingers touch the sensitive hollow before his hand winds beneath my hair and around the back of my neck.

He applies pressure, bringing my lips to his in a soft but demanding kiss. Even though I'm tall for a woman, I have to rise on my tiptoes to reach him. I steady myself, accidentally digging my fingernails into the skin of his muscled chest. His indrawn breath at the sharp little pain is the first sound either of us has made. I moan in response.

His tongue splits the seam of my lips, delving into my mouth, coaxing a response that I wholeheartedly want to give in to. Passion explodes between us when he understands I'm on board. His kiss becomes rougher, hotter, needier. I bite his lip, sucking, and gnawing at his mouth, unwilling to give him the lead. I want him to take it.

My heart skips a beat as his other hand wraps around my waist, pushing into the small of my back to bring me flush against him. His hardness presses into my lower stomach, and I raise one knee, sliding it up his hard, thick thigh. I can't lift it any higher, so I wind my ankle around his leg, locking him to me. On the periphery, lightning flashes.

A low rumble starts in his chest beneath my hands, more felt than heard. He pulls his lips from mine with a sexy growl. He tips me backward, bending my spine. He runs his nose down the side of my throat to the hollow notch at its base. He takes in a deep breath through his nose, drawing in my scent, before pushing aside the neckline of my shirt and running first his lips and then his nose over the swell of my left breast. Fire and brimstone fly, creating deep craters as they meet the ground, but I barely notice.

Deliberately, he sinks his teeth into the side of my breast. Opening his mouth wide, he pulls the flesh between his lips and marks me by sucking. Hard. I gasp, writhing in his arms as the fiery sting of blood is sucked to the surface of my skin, mingling with the heat of his hot, moist mouth. Thunder rumbles and rolls across the plain on which we stand, shaking the ground beneath our feet.

Scrabbling for some sort of control, I sink my hands into his silken hair, feeling thin braids on both sides of his head. I'm about to speak, to beg him to take me, when he rears back, roaring in pain. We sink in what seems like slow motion to the ground. I grab his shoulders as his weight presses down on me. I watch as his beautiful eyes dim and then drift closed. It's then that I realize both of us are covered in his blood.

Chapter 2

Nola

Bang. Bang. Bang!

I can't seem to open my eyes. There's a heavy weight on them holding them closed.

I can hear muffled voices. Some whispering, some blustering.

Bang. Bang. Bang!

"Wha...the fu...?"

What's going on? I blink, trying to open my eyes. My mouth is dry, my muscles cramped, and the room is fuzzy, but I can make out the soft gray blackout curtains and sky-blue paint on the walls. The open closet door is familiar. Jasmine always forgets to shut it, but this scene isn't what I expect to see. I raise my hand to rub my eye, but stop. I want to avoid getting blood in my eyes. Except, there is no trace of blood on the hand in front of my face.

Even though I know I won't see him here, I lift my head, turning it side to side, looking around for him anyway. I have a burning need to know if he's all right. It doesn't matter that I don't know him. It doesn't matter that I almost had sex with a stranger, it doesn't matter that it was only a dream. A vision. What matters is that on a cellular level, I know this man is somehow a part of me. Always has been and always will be.

Bang. Bang. Bang!

I startle. I'm not certain if it's because someone is hammering on our door or if it's because of that last thought. Any kind of interaction with this man is going to have to be a big resounding no! I'm not opening myself up to that kind of hurt, not now, not ever. Besides, it's not like I'll ever meet him. Right? Right?

"Ah shit. Fucking visions." Weak as a kitten, I struggle to slide my legs off the bed and sit up. "And who the hell is making all that racket?" I grumble.

"Nola?" Jasmine half whispers as she slinks into our room. "Oh, thank God. You're awake! You're okay?"

I wave my hand, neither confirming nor denying her question, but just as quickly drop it back to the bed. I'm woozy as hell. Not only that, but I feel like I went on a good bender. I wish I could just go back to sleep and forget what and who I saw in the vision. Knowing that isn't possible, I'll deal with whatever is happening now. "What's going on?"

"William Roberts and his ass-kissers are outside, demanding we let them in."

"Great, just what we need." I drag in a deep breath. Maybe more oxygen will keep my head from spinning. I sigh. "Help me up."

Once I'm on my feet, I shuffle to the closet and pull a pair of sweatpants off the shelf. Steadying myself against the doorjamb, I get one leg in, but then stumble and nearly face plant on the floor when my other foot gets caught in the fabric. Once I finally get them on, I lift the handgun stored there off the shelf and check the magazine before closing the closet door and smoothing my empty hand over my hair.

"Let's go see what BAP wants this time." I slowly make my way out of our room and down the short hallway, with her trailing behind me. I keep the gun concealed along the outside of my thigh and hidden by my T-shirt. Ginger and Tanni are huddled together in the kitchen nook. "You armed?" I ask. Both nod.

"BAP?" Jasmine questions.

"Yeah. Big. Ass. Problem." Jasmine's guffaw brings a small smile to my lips. "What time is it?"

"Around eight o'clock. Why? You got somewhere you need to be?" She giggles again. I don't answer her because I've reached the door.

"Open it, but only a few inches, and keep your foot pressed against the bottom. I don't trust him, so be prepared for anything. Okay?"

Jasmine flips the tumblers on the three locks before pulling the door open about twelve inches and braces her foot at the bottom.

"What?" I ask, glaring at William Roberts and his two goons.

"Now, that's not a neighborly way to answer the door, Nola," he chastises.

"Oh? You're moving in?" The house closest to us is a piece of shit. The roof has fallen in, and the yard is full of junk and weeds. I know he's just trying to put me in my place by being the big man and all.

"Not hardly." He sneers. "We're here"—he points at my door—"to inform you we've taken a vote in town. I'm the new mayor. All citizens will be required to pay a tax in goods or *services* starting today." And then he has the audacity to wink.

"A vote, huh? I wonder why this is the first I'm hearing about this act of democracy taking place." I raise my voice so that Ginger and Tanni can hear me too. "Girls, you hear anything about electing a mayor?"

"Nope."

"Nuh-uh."

"I sure didn't."

"Yeah. We didn't hear about a vote, Roberts, sorry." I give him a thin, insincere smile. I cock my head and squint my eyes a bit and let them go unfocused as I look over his left shoulder. He scuffs his boots but otherwise doesn't move. The men behind him must be smarter than he is, because each takes a healthy step back. "I don't... *We* don't acknowledge you as any type of authority in this town, especially as mayor, but I'll do you a favor and give you the *only* service any of us has to offer, and I'll make it free just this once, us being neighbors and all."

Even though I feel like a pile of steaming dog shit, I give him my best smile. He smirks, the asshat, thinking he's won.

"Well now, I knew you could be friendly if you put your mind to it." He hooks his thumbs into his belt loops so his fingers practically cup his penis from both sides. I barely contain the eye roll.

"You're gonna die. Slowly and painfully. Electrocution, I think. Maybe lightning? Your eyeballs are gonna pop right out of your head like little blackened coals." I add a dramatic shudder. "It isn't pretty, but it is coming for *you*. Best get prepared to meet your maker, William Roberts."

"Wha...?"

"You heard me. You grew up in the same town as me. You *know* what I can do. Not only that, but you *know* if I say it, it's gonna happen. Here's the most important thing: you and your goons are gonna leave us alone. You don't pressure us. You don't look at us. Furthermore, you don't talk to us, because if you do? I'll do everything within my power to make sure it happens much sooner rather than later. Understand?" I don't wait for his agreement. Instead, I close the door in his face and Jasmine throws the locks.

"It's time," I tell the other girls as I turn around. "We'll pack up and start heading north by the end of the week for that city that welcomes humans, the one those travelers who came through a couple of months ago mentioned."

Truex

Unsettled by the erotic and turbulent dream, I wake earlier than my brethren. I am disturbed by the tumultuous situation growing in Tellus and the remnants of the beguiling woman in my dream from the night before. If she is real, is she in danger?

Did I, in my mind's eye, see her in the streets yesterday and not consciously notice her? I doubt it. One of the warriors would have surely noticed her extraordinary demeanor and bearing, if not her singular appearance.

She was regal. Statuesque. With her crown of tiny braids surrounding her head and flowing down her back in a waterfall of color ranging from rich black soil to sun-kissed wheat, she would draw attention to herself. We would have all noticed.

Her skin, not golden, but lightly burnished with a warm caramel patina, was flawless. Her dark, almost black eyes hint at another color but within the gloom and mist surrounding us. I could not discern it even though they held centuries of wisdom, a sharp intellect, and yes, a wealth of weariness, pain, and wariness that spoke directly to my soul.

She is a figment of my imagination, yet I feel she is part of me. A missing piece. A piece I must find. For without her, I am incomplete. It makes no sense. How can I find a woman I have only seen and felt in a dream? I must be losing my mind. We have been isolated and indolent for too long.

Enough of this nonsense! Pushing to my feet, I take care of my morning ablutions before going to the fire. I notice my prince is awake, and the others issue small complaints as they too wake for the day.

"If one were to judge by the moans and groans, I would say we woke in a contingent of females and not the royal guard. What say you, Orion?" I grumble as I offer my prince a steaming fragrant cup of tea and continue to try to shake off the arousing dream from last night.

He grins in response as he accepts my offering, but he seems preoccupied. Ribald comments and laughter are bandied about as the warriors play their normal practical jokes and our camp comes fully awake. I am glad for the distraction, even though I do not participate further.

Out of the southern darkness, the hair-raising vibrations of what must be a banshee's cry wash over the camp. It is a powerful dirge of death and challenge, freezing me for a moment with its power.

Shaking off the sudden inertia, I leap to protect my prince.

"By all that is sacred, *what was that?*" Jahzuah's awed whisper adds to the tension.

"That, warriors, is my mate," our prince announces with utmost conviction.

By the Lady! A resounding tremor rocks through my entire body. It's as if someone has struck a massive gong inside me. I shudder and shake, losing track of the surrounding conversation as I try to keep my legs from collapsing beneath me. Mate? Is it possible? The prince's declaration ignites a spark of recognition deep within me.

Something inside me quivers with excitement, yet also settles at the thought.

"We need a plan," my prince declares.

We damned sure do!

The plan is for Tarrik, Ronan, Basil, Carson, Rylan, and me to split off from the prince and the rest of the elite guard so we can cover more ground. One group will go west around the outskirts of the Waste, covering the towns and villages along the way, while the other group goes east. Both with the intention of gathering survivors and refugees and encouraging them to come north where there is plenty of food, safety, and assistance. We will meet at the bottom and work our way back together, hopefully with the prince's mate in tow.

I do not mention that my mate may be out here, that is, until we are away from the main group.

"Tarrik?" I look up at the stars, impatient to see if she will visit me in my dreams again this eve. Part of me prays she will, but most of me is afraid she will not. If not, what will I do? It was a dream. Is she even real? How can I be so invested already?

"Yeah?"

I swallow hard, unsure of how to tell him, of how he will react. Will he believe me?

"Just say it." He blows out a frustrated sigh.

"I had a dream... I think my mate is out here somewhere too. I feel this connection. A visceral pull. The only time I've ever felt like this is when you and I are away from each other." I hold my breath, waiting for him to respond.

"Is that what has been going on with you as of late? I was going to bring it up, but I wanted to give you time to sort out your discontentment. You've been distracted lately. Tell me about the dream, brother."

I release a breath and tell him as much of the dream as I can remember, how regal and beautiful she was. How I felt with her in my arms, and how I felt upon waking to realize it wasn't real. "What do you think?"

"*I think* you two should stop whispering like little girls and shut up. If destiny has chosen a mate for you, count yourself lucky. Her? Maybe not so much." Ronan, using a stage whisper, joins our conversation.

Carson, Rylan, and Basil chuckle, our private conversation is obviously not so private after all.

"Seriously, my friend, get some sleep. Our prince and now you have given the rest of us the spark of hope we need to keep going. This isolation has been hard on us all. Have no worry, we will help you find your lady." Ronan's advice is sound, but I still lay awake for hours, imagining the possibilities.

Nola

"Are we going to talk about it?" Jasmine asks as we fill up the last of three gas cans we found. Hopefully, the gas is good, or we're going to be hoofing it instead of driving in style. That style being a vintage black two-door Cadillac.

"Talk about what?"

"Don't play dumb. It's been three days since the *episode*." She puts the word in air quotes and gives me the patented *you're being a dumbass* look.

"I don't know, Jasmine." I sigh, checking the level in the can as we continue to siphon out the fuel. "I think this one has me more freaked out than the one that started all this."

"How so? Come on, girl, talk to me." Jasmine is the closest thing I've ever had to caring family, and she has her own psychic demons to deal with, so I give in. At least I don't see dead people. *Thank goodness.* She doesn't have to push me all that hard because it's been weighing on me and I could use a fresh perspective.

"It started out all eerie and misty, but then I felt this presence connecting to me, and a bird appeared out of the mist and turned into this seriously intense, smokin'-hot dude. He took me into his arms and ravaged me...and I ravaged right back."

Jasmine stares at me, mouth open, eyes wide, awed wonder written all over her face. "Girl, are you telling me your vision was a wet dream? You were getting it on with some hot god? Was it Loki? No. No wait! Odin is the one with the crows, right? Did you get it on with the *All-Father*? The old man?" Her laughter shakes the can, sloshing the gas, so I push her aside and takeover both tasks.

"No, you idiot. He was *young* and hot. No dad or gramp bod in sight." I suppress the eye roll, barely, but I can feel my eyeballs straining with the effort. "Are you done? Do you want to hear the rest or not?"

"There's more?"

"Yeah, there's more." I slip my thumb over the end of the siphoning hose before tipping it into the air and pulling it from the holding tank at a deserted farm a mile or so from town. Jasmine twists the cap onto the can while I loop the hose and recap the tank.

"Well?"

God, this girl is impatient. I help her lift the can into the carriage. We work together to turn it around and begin pushing it back toward town. "Well, while we were trying our damnedest to get into each other's pants, it started to storm. Thunder, lightning, fire, and brimstone flying, but we hardly noticed. I don't know if he noticed at all. All of a sudden, he throws his head back, screaming in pain. We're both covered in blood and falling to the ground. He was hurt, but he next thing I know, I'm waking up to BAP pounding on our door."

We trudge down the long driveway, me pushing and her pulling and lifting the creaking and groaning baby carriage over the ruts and up onto the pitted asphalt in complete silence while she absorbs what I've said, and I relive that last scene again.

"What do you think happened?" She's much more subdued as she grunts and yanks the carriage over a particularly rough spot in the road. "Do you want me to *ask?*"

I worry for a minute that it might not make this one last trip with all the weight we have in it. We just might wind up having to carry the cans over the strange, melded terrain. In some spots, it would be easier, but it's a long walk, and the weirdness of overlap of earth and this new realm makes it difficult. The asphalt turning into an open field with strange plant-life only lasts for a hundred yards or so in this spot, but we have a few more to contend with up ahead.

"I don't know. Nothing good, that's for sure." I sigh. "I don't think the spirits of the dead can tell you anything, and it's probably not a smart idea here to go stirring things up, especially if there are other beings' spirits too." So much about this new realm is still up in the air. We know so little about the other species and creatures, only what I've seen. The other girls are aware we aren't alone here. I'm still upset about the vision, but talking to Jasmine settles me a bit. We need to proceed with caution, and Jasmine communing with spirits isn't cautious at all.

"So, when do you think we'll meet him? Do you think he'll know you? What if you're the only one to experience the dream? What if he's married? What are you going to do? You always said there weren't going to be any relationships for you, so what's the plan?" She's throwing out questions faster than I can answer them. Questions I've asked myself a thousand times over the last few days. Questions I still don't have answers to.

"Honestly? I don't know."

Chapter 3

"Nola? We've been thinking," Ginger says just before popping a piece of rustic Italian bread into her mouth. The bread is a celebratory treat we made with our dwindling supply of flour. Space is limited, so we can't take everything with us, unless we find a way to pull something behind the Caddy. Without a ball and hitch or a trailer, that option isn't going to happen.

"Yeah? What's up?"

"Well, think we should have something to trade. I mean, you have your readings but we"—she points to Tanni and Jasmine—"don't have any marketable skills or a product we can trade with. Yeah, we could offer lap dances, but we're not prostitutes, and we prefer not to go down that road. It was bad enough when we danced for a living, but now? No."

I see her point. Lost in thought, I watch as honey oozes off my bread in a slow, sticky drip onto my pinkie finger. A month or so ago, Jasmine had noticed the bees on the flowers beside the road as we were searching for supplies. Bees need water, so we followed them, hoping to find their source. What we found instead was a honey tree.

"Tanni, how many jars with lids would you say we have?" I lick the sticky drop from the tip of my finger.

"Well, we kept all the pint jars and lids from the jams we made and ate. I think we have three boxes at twelve a box, so that's what, thirty-six jars? Why?"

"What if we collected honey from the tree? Those three boxes wouldn't take up too much space in the trunk. You'd have something of value to barter."

"Do you think we could?" Ginger's voice lilts with excitement.

"What if we get stung?" Tanni, ever cautious, asks.

"It's worth a try, isn't it?" Jasmine chimes in.

"I guess we won't know until we try. Let's prep the jars and find a bucket or two. Do we still have that burlap from the garden in the garage? We can smoke the bees if we need to, but last time, they didn't bother us. We'll go in the morning, okay?"

"I'm sorry. Are you sure you're all right?" Tanni struggles, waddling like a duck with the five-gallon bucket between her legs as she moves it out of the bushes and away from the hive.

"It's not that bad. I'll put some baking soda on when we get back to the house. Just don't swat at any more of them." I follow closely behind her until I can grab a hold of the handle, so we're both carrying the heavy pail.

I probably wouldn't have gotten stung at all if she hadn't panicked and started swatting at them. It's a good thing I was ready with the burlap and a lighter. Smoke interferes with a bee's sense of smell. They don't react to pheromones that cause alarm. It doesn't hurt them, and the hive was big, so we left plenty for their survival too.

"Good Lord! I'm glad we don't have too far to go. Can you imagine carrying this all the way from the farm?" she asks as we awkwardly stumble down the road with the bucket between us.

"No," I puff, already winded. "This baby has got to weigh at least fifty pounds."

"Let's stop and switch sides. This handle is killing my hand." We clumsily plop the bucket on the road. It's good that honey doesn't slosh, or most of it would wind up on the ground, and we'd be back to square one. "What's that noise?"

"I don't hear anything." I glance around us and then farther out at the horizon.

"It sounds like...a flock of crows."

"Crows?" A frisson of excitement zings though my veins, distracting me from telling her a flock of crows is called a murder. Are the crows coincidental? Maybe a sign? "I haven't seen any around since things changed, but that doesn't mean anything. Look at the bees. Come on, switch sides with me and let's get home."

The rest of the way, we don't hear anything. When we get home, Jasmine and Ginger are nowhere to be found, but I'm not worried. They probably went to town for gossip and to see what the BAP's been up to since I cursed him.

Tanni and I set about melting the wax of the top of the honeycomb with a chef's knife we heated. We drain the honey before placing a piece of the honeycomb into each jar and ladling the honey over it. Tanni lets out a squeal of fright as both Jasmine and Ginger barrel through the door, and I almost overpour the jar I'm filling.

"You guys are not gonna believe this!" Ginger gushes.

"He's here." Jasmine meets my startled gaze, her voice much more subdued in volume, but intense.

"What? Who's here? What's going on?" Confusion washes over Tanni's face. I know exactly what they're talking about.

"Nola's dream man. He's here."

"How do you know?" I whisper.

"Gorgeous, intense, powerful? Roberts is trying to run them off, telling them there isn't anyone else in the area and to move along. They're looking for someone."

"They?"

"Oh yeah. Two of them look exactly alike, but the other four are all similar. *All hotties!*" Ginger snickers as she polishes her knuckles on her shirt. "Do you realize how long it's been since we've seen a fine-looking man? I mean, I'd never go there, but Roberts was even beginning to look good."

"Eww!"

"Gross."

"That's disgusting!"

"What? He's not bad looking, he's just an asshole." Ginger crosses her arms over her chest, defending her position.

"He's got a wife. Emma that poor girl, has to put up with all of his chauvinistic disgustingness," Tanni chimes in. "We gonna go to town and at least ogle these hot men? It sure would be nice to be on the other side of the stage for once."

"I don't know. Let's get this honey put up first, and then we'll decide." We make short work of the last few jars and pack them away into the boxes. We want to avoid loading them in the car tonight in case it gets stolen; we'll load them in the morning.

When I finish with the last box, I find all three of them staring at me, and I sigh.

"Okay, let me grab my cards." I also wash my face and run a hand over my braids, deciding at the last second to add a colorful blue boho bandeau wrap to my head.

"Nola knows all, tells all. Good way to break the ice or scare someone off," Jasmine teases.

Looking right at me, Ginger scolds us, "Roberts has probably kicked them out of town. Let's go already. I need some interaction. The sexy male kind!" Typical of her normal *let's get shit done yesterday* rushing behavior, she yanks open the front door and slams into a giant body standing right on the doorstep.

"How fortuitous. I am, of course, at your service, sweetling."

Truex

"There is a small village with a handful of occupants," Rylan reports with a wave of his hand in the general direction of where he has been reconning. "Maybe a dozen or so."

Tarrik nods, donning his sage persona. He even folds his hands calmly in front of himself. "Then that is where we shall go. How should we approach?"

"From what I observed as I flew over, it is mostly men. Observing under glamour may be a wise choice." Rylan crunches into an apple, wiping juice from his chin.

"Aggressive?" I ask.

"Hmm, not toward each other. Maybe dominant? The few women I saw seemed to be doing all the heavy chores. Washing, gathering, and the like." He tosses the core and grabs a piece of pemmican.

"Perhaps we could use the stones we are looking for to break the ice? I never saw the inner workings of the Omnichronos or the Omniport, for that matter, and the image Cormac showed us could easily be mistaken for something else," Basil adds.

"Why don't we go in and demand to see the women? If my mate is there, I will just take her, and we can be on our way," I grumble. I'm impatient to find her, and all this planned diplomacy is a pain in the ass.

"What about the prince's mate?" Basil asks.

Ronan adds to the conundrum. "We do not know if his mate is even female. How will we distinguish her from another?"

Destiny has given us a monumental task by adding a mate hunt to an already wild-goose chase.

"We'll make all of them come with us. Male and female. They won't be able to thrive or even survive out here much longer anyway." If I must force every single Human on Lykosian to move north, then that is what I'll do.

Tarrik lays out the plan. "All right. We will go in under the glamour of crows, observe, and then reconvene before going in as warriors."

It is just like him to throw out a question, let everyone else debate it, and then lay out a plan that he was probably going to offer up from the beginning. He's wily that way, allowing everyone to think they actually had a hand in making the decision. It's what makes him a good second to Jahzuah. He's the calm. I'm the chaos. At least that is what he would like you to think. In reality, I'm the thunderstorm—loud, destructive, but quickly diminished. He's a hurricane—it takes days for him to build, but once he reaches full capacity, he leaves utter destruction in his wake. People rarely see it, so they forget it is there.

I am more of an enforcer. I get in, get shit handled, and maybe ask questions after. Not only that, but I just want to get moving. This "sit around and talk shit to death" is making me itchy and irritable.

"Can we please go now?" Yup, there it is, the impatience I'm famous for.

"Yes." Tarrik smirks. Asshole. He was deliberately drawing it out. He thinks this is humorous.

"Just wait," I warn him. "When you finally find your mate, I pray to the Lady that she is a harridan and runs you in circles before she accepts your claim!"

"Do not put that out there," he warns.

"Too late. It is what it is, so say I."

"So, mote it be," Ronan gravely confirms, sealing the prayer, giving weight to it in spirit.

Tarrik glares, his unflappable demeanor finally ruffled. Shared laughter at his expense alleviates a bit of the tension, but I'm still chomping at the bit to get moving.

I sit quietly in the shade of a tall steeple. Observing this little village is a revelation. There are only a few people, but the males are lazy. While five women do all the work, from gardening to carrying water to washing clothing to cooking on the outdoor fire, the men laze around, talking to each other and making demands of the women. One male in particular enjoys being the boss. He is especially rude to the woman who has been waiting on him.

The only thing I haven't seen the women do is cut wood for the fires, but they were hauling it. Disgusted, I shake my feathers. I've had enough. I take to the sky, calling out to my brethren.

Tarrik is the first to join me in a copse of trees that are a mix of the fruit-bearing Polzia tree of Tellus and some sort of hardwood from the earth realm. The earth trees are towering and statuesque. The leaves are still intact but have browned to a golden sienna. The branches also hold little round nuts with funny little caps on them. Plucking a few, I slip them into a pocket to carry back to Cormac at Summer's Veil.

"The way they treat their females is shameful," Basil says as he lands.

"It is," I agree.

"I counted eight men lazing about or working on some sort of metallic contraptions, two boys cutting wood, and five women doing the majority of the work." Ronan, who was under an invisibility glamour at street level, has the most to offer by way of information.

"We will walk into this village. If we need an excuse, we will ask about the stones." Tarrik gives each of us a level look. "I will do the talking."

As a group, we take up an arrow formation, with Tarrik in the lead and me to the right and a step or two behind him. The rest of the warriors fall into position behind us.

The first to notice us is the female who was being berated earlier. She stops, mouth hanging open, and stares until the male who acts as if he is in charge bellows at her for standing in the street. She says something to him, and he finally looks our way. He must snap at her, because she turns and hurries into the dwelling he is sitting in front of.

An older woman carrying a bucket of water stops short, sloshing the contents on her shoes. Basil breaks off from our group to take the bucket from her before offering his other arm as escort. She doesn't move. She just stands there staring at him in the same manner as the first female.

The man finally stands, hitching his pants around a waist that is heading toward fat. He's more powerfully built in the chest, but it is obvious he has done little physical labor.

"State your business," he orders us. I catch a flash of motion in my periphery, but when I turn to look at the two closely spaced dwellings, nothing is there. Rylan nods, letting me know he has seen it too.

Tarrik steps forward, "I am Tarrik, second captain of the elite guard of Prince Orion of Elfame. We have been sent on a quest from our prince."

"A prince, huh? What's the quest?"

"Our prince is searching for his mate. He also looks for precious stones from the earth realm. It is also our duty to invite the survivors of the cataclysm to travel north where it is safer, and the land more prosperous. You will travel under our protection, of course."

The gleam that enters this man's eyes at the mention of our prince does not go unnoticed by me, and I am sure not by any of the warriors watching him.

"His mate, you say. Would there be a reward for helping find this mate? Or perhaps the stones you're looking for?"

"Perhaps." Tarrik, ever the diplomat, answers with a regal tilt of his head. "How may I address you, sir?"

The man stands a little taller, puffing up his chest and lifting his chin. He likes being treated as a man of power.

"I'm the mayor. Roberts, William Roberts.

"How many people do you have here in your village, Roberts, William Roberts?"

By the look on the man's face, Tarrik has somehow disconcerted him. "Well, uh, ah-hem. There are the men and the boys, so ten."

"And the females?"

"There's five of those, but they're not relevant."

A feminine voice interjects from within the open doorway behind Roberts, William Roberts, making his face turn red. "Those are whores and a witch. They're not part of our community!"

"They're not whores, they're just women," the female voice contradicts. She's deep within the shadowed interior so I can't see her, but her voice reaches past him to where we stand.

Roberts's face flushes purple as anger washes over his features. "Get back to your chores!"

"There are more than five females here?" Tarrik asks the disgruntled man.

"There are four more, but you won't want anything to do with them. Loose morals. Into witchcraft, casting spells and curses. Man haters, every one of them, worthless cunts!"

I grunt in surprise at the derogatory slur. I've already formed the opinion that he has no regard for females of his species, but since he would use such vile language toward a female, my dislike for him grows exponentially.

The Fae is a matriarchal society. We warriors take our strength and direction from our queen. That our queen is gone has grieved us sorely. That he would take the stance he has against females puts him squarely into the category of the untrustworthy and as a probable enemy.

"We will make our camp on the outskirts of your town, Roberts, William Roberts. If you and your followers"—Tarrik indicates the rest of the men and the boys gathering—"would like to discuss preparations for accompanying us when we depart, we will be at the copse of mixed trees outside your village."

"It's just Roberts, or you can call me Mayor."

"As you wish." Tarrik bows and turns away. Each of us follows suit.

We stop and wait as Basil escorts the older female to her destination. He tips his head down, listening to her as they walk. When he rejoins us, he whispers, "I know the location of the other females."

Excitement buzzes through my veins like bees around a fragrant flower. The tension in me is almost tangible. Tarrik must feel it through our twin connection because he winks at me and says, "Well done. Basil, certainly lead the way."

Nola

"Shit."

"Oh. My. God."

"Well...hello."

My roommates can articulate their surprise, but I can't even whisper a word. My mouth dries up, my lips grow numb, and my hands begin to quiver. The tarot cards break free of my suddenly nerveless fingers and flutter to the floor at my feet, their silken wrap drifting behind them. For once in my life, I'm indecisive. I know I should take actions to defend someone breaching our home, our sanctuary, but I can't hear, I can't reason. I can't move except for the shaking that's taken over my muscles.

My knees weaken as big bodies push through the doorway, filling up our small front room. I feel like we're being invaded by an army, but, there are probably only five or six of them.

I'm unable to meet any of their eyes. Likewise, I'm afraid that the man from my dream is with them, and I'm terrified to discover that he isn't.

My knees turn to liquid, threatening to collapse, spilling me onto the floor. I glance down, expecting to fall. My precious life-saving cards lay scattered across the floor, about to be trampled on by heavy feet. Only two are faceup. The first is the Wheel of Fortune and the second is the King of Swords looking back at me.

I drop to my knees, thankful to have something to do. Thankful to avoid the attention coming my way. Thankful that my frozen, trembling hands work as I gather the cards one by one and carefully form a neat and precise deck.

"May I help?"

I shiver at the deep, sexy timbre. The skein of multicolored hand-painted silk appears in front of me. I reach out and grasp it, but he doesn't let go. His skin is hot beneath my cold fingers. Surprised, I raise my eyes to him, and the rest of the world falls away as I stare into the deepest blue eyes. Eyes that I've seen only in my vision. I'm lost in his gaze as we kneel there, tarot cards stacked on the floor between us, both of us holding on to that piece of silk. It feels like a lifeline to me. I have the strangest urge to ask if it's the same for him.

I know this man. Not only that, but I've kissed him, almost had sex with him. It was a vision, but we almost had sex. Sex! I release his gaze, letting mine drift over his body, maybe subconsciously looking for the blood that interrupted us. I reach out the hand holding the scarf, lifting his own with mine, and place it on his chest. His hand shifts, covering mine, holding it pressed against his heart, and I realize I've voluntarily touched him.

My eyes jerk to his in surprise for the second time in as many minutes. His are heated, but a soft smile plays against his beautifully sculpted mouth. With my hand still resting against him, he helps me to rise.

"Hold out your other hand," he whispers. I raise my free hand. With the softness of butterfly wings, he places the deck on my palm, the King of Swords still faceup.

"Th-thank you," I whisper.

"You are welcome, my mate."

Chapter 4

N^{ola}

His what? Can this really be happening? His face is exactly as I remember it, but in the vision, I couldn't read his thoughts. Well, I can't now either, but somehow, I have an inkling of how he's feeling. The current of electricity running between us feels like I'm touching a live wire. It feeds me information and clues me in to his turbulent emotions.

Hope, joy, wonderment, fear, desire, and so much more race along the link between us, radiating outward and filling the surrounding space.

His smell is the same, delicious and warm. The heady mixture of sandalwood, clove, and citrus is much stronger now than in the vision, and if that doesn't blow my mind, I'm not sure what else can. It's ridiculous, but I can't help but lean forward and pull more of his beguiling scent deep within me. My eyes drift closed, my face almost tucked into his neck. His free arm loops around my waist, pulling me closer to him until I rest against him completely. I sigh, lost in the presence and essence of the man before me.

A small gasp jerks me back to the here and now. I step back from him. Heat rushes into my cheeks when I notice everyone is quietly watching us. His big body moves as he places himself between me and the rest of the room. That he would protect me, giving me privacy, melts a small piece of my icy heart, but this, whatever it is, cannot be.

"Come with me." Taking my hand, he tugs until I follow him across the room and out the door. We're a few yards away from the house when I realize I'm blindly trailing after him. *I don't know him. I don't even know his name!*

"Wait. Stop. I don't know you. I can't just walk off with you all willy-nilly!" I dig in my heels, refusing to move one step further.

"Willy-nilly?" He grins. "You do know me, my flame. I wish for us to learn more about each other without an audience present." He bends, putting his shoulder into my stomach, and lifts me off the ground before walking down the street with me slung over him like a bag of dirty laundry.

"You did not just do that!" I gasp. "Put me down or so help me...awk!" His hand lands against my butt with a resounding smack as he ambles off through the rubble and tall grasses. "Why you...you...barbarian! Who do you think you are? Put me down!"

I'm tempted to pound on him, but my tarot cards are still in one hand. Oh, to hell with this! A red wave of anger and something more tantalizing that I'm choosing to ignore washes over me. With all my might, I pound my empty fist against his ass cheek over and over. Frustrated, I open my mouth to scream because hitting him obviously isn't working. Suddenly, I have a better idea. I can feel the evil grin pulling at my lips. If I could rub my hands together in anticipation, I would. I push the hair out of my face and slump against his back. He grunts his approval. The idiot probably thinks I've given up, but I haven't. Instead, I sink my teeth into his shirt and skin, biting down. Hard!

"Aaaiiiieee! By the Lady, let loose, you cannibal!" He shakes and then rolls me off his shoulder.

My feet hit the ground with jarring intensity. The bandeau holding back my hair falls to the dirt. My head swims from going from upside down to right side up in a blink of the eye. I glare up at him through the braids that have swung into my face.

His eyes smolder back at me, first with ire, and then with something much hotter. Something much more dangerous. Lust.

I rock back a step, but it's too late. His chiseled lips are on mine, blazing a trail of fire through my resistance and obliterating my common sense.

I throw myself into the kiss. It's like hurtling off a cliff in free fall and praying the water is deep enough beneath you. I pull him closer and push him away, fighting for control with my tongue, teeth, and lips. Our hands tangle in each other's hair, hostile and angry. I moan with the pleasure that it brings me, and once again, I lose myself to his dominating flame.

Like any flash fire, our passion burns hot and quick before settling into embers that are warm, glowing, comforting. I come back to myself, amazed that we're still standing, astonished our clothes are still on our bodies. Which is a good thing because we're standing in an open field where anyone can see us.

"Oh, holy shit!" I whisper as I bring my fingers to my lips. "What *was* that?" I've never allowed anyone to get under my skin. I've never allowed anyone to get that close. Furthermore, I've never allowed anyone to affect my emotions to the point of rage or to the point of bliss. And in just that one kiss, I've experienced both simultaneously.

I'm stunned. The connection between us feels precious, boundless, and unstoppable, but therein lies the illusion. My visions do not lie. If I love this man, I will lose him, and it will break me faster, harder, and more completely than anything in my past ever has. If I allow this to happen, it will destroy me completely.

I gaze into his eyes filled with the remnants of passion as well as deep-seated conviction. I whisper the only thing that makes sense. The only thing that might save me. "No."

Truex

"Yes." I refuse to take no for an answer. She is mine and I am hers. Destiny has deemed it so.

"You don't understand!"

"Then tell me. But first, may I have the name of the woman I am destined to love?"

"Oh my God! You can't love me! I've kissed you, let you carry me off, abandoned my friends, and I don't even know your name! This is insane!"

It is startling to see her so upset. Somehow, I thought she would be as excited as I am, but she is quite distressed. I thought my words of commitment would be pleasing to her. Do not all women want those words? The fact is, they seem to have the opposite effect. How can I get to the bottom of this if she will not speak with me? She is unwilling to even share her name.

"Please?" I beg softly. My normal storm-the-gates attitude will not work with her. I need to understand her resistance. "Please." I reach out and brush just the tips of our fingers together. The sigh she releases is so deep, so saddened, so defeated. What has she been through? And why, by the Lady, did I not search for her sooner?

"Nola. My name is Nola."

"Thank you. It is my pleasure to meet you, Nola. I am Truex." Maybe a little conversation will soften her. "How is it that you walked in my dream?" Wariness washes over her features as she crosses her arms, hunching as she holds on to herself tightly. Does she feel she must hold herself together lest she fly to pieces at any moment?

"I've never done it before...walked into someone else's dream..."

"What have you done, Nola?" I love the sound of her name on my lips. It is sensual and exotic and fits her perfectly. Physically, she is everything I hoped for and nothing like I could have imagined.

She's irritated, but then her face smooths, dropping all emotion. She stiffens, standing straight and tall, her bearing regal and strong. "I have visions."

"...and you saw me? Came to me?"

"I didn't know it was you. I wish it wasn't."

Her words hit me like a blow to my stomach. My heart aches as I raise my hand, rubbing at my chest. She does not want me. She is tearing me apart.

"Is there someone else, then, who holds your affection? I do not understand. Destiny has brought us together. We are mates."

"No! Of course, there isn't anyone else. Why would you think that? And what do you mean we're destined to be together?"

"Destiny, kismet, fate. Take your pick. It has been written in the stars that you and I are mates. A matched pair. How do you not know this?"

"I'm human. I'm not sure what you are, but most humans can't be faithful and honest with each other to save their lives!"

Once again, I am stunned by the blow she delivers.

"You would not be faithful?"

"What? No! Of course, I can be faithful, but I *lived* with how my father treated my mom and me. I *saw* the men my mom would get so excited about when they entered her life and how devastated she was when they left. I would never treat someone that way!"

Ah, now we get to the crux of the whole misunderstanding. She has been hurt, damaged by those who should have cared for her and loved her best. I will have to tread carefully to help her unravel these snares that keep her in bondage.

"I am your destined mate. We have a connection." I wave my hand between us. "You can sense the things I feel, just as I can sense yours. Neither of us can put the other aside or cuckold the other. We are a matched pair, two pieces of the same whole. Do you understand?"

I reach for her again, taking her delicate hand into my own and cradling it with gentleness.

"Do you understand and believe me? How else would you have connected with me in a vision, Nola?"

Tears form in her eyes and spill down her cheeks. There is something holding her back. I can feel fear coursing through our connection.

"Please, tell me. Share this burden with me, as mates are supposed to do."

"Oh God! It's not that I don't want you. It's not that I don't feel this." Her finger dances back and forth between us. "Whatever it is, I do! I just can't!"

"Why not?" I growl, fed up with not knowing the dilemma. Unable to fix what she cannot seem to explain, I get angry. "Why not?" I shout.

"Because!" she shouts back. "I'll become attached to you, and then you'll die on me! I've seen it! You'll leave me, just like everyone else always...has." The dam holding back her emotions not only cracks, it shatters. Great racking sobs pour from her mouth. Tears run in rivulets down her beautiful but reddening face. She turns away, but I grab her, pulling her into my arms.

I run my hand over her braids, holding her close to me. I make soothing sounds against her temple. I do not know what to do. Why would she think this? What did she see? I am at a loss.

"Is everything all right, brother?" *Oh, thank the Lady!* Tarrik will help me figure this out.

Nola buries her face deeper into my shoulder. My already wet shirt sticks to my skin, but I ignore the discomfort. Her dismay at being out of control radiates between us but is overridden by the grief flowing from her into me. I pull in a shaky breath, fighting to keep a firm grasp on my control. I want to help her weather this storm, but the emotional vibration between us erodes what little restraint I have been able to maintain.

"Nola? Nola, please, sweetling. Please, your tears are killing me." I rock her back and forth. She is tall for a woman but feels slight in my arms. I whisper nonsense to her, offering up the comfort of my strength. As with any highly emotional state, it cannot be maintained for any length of time and the torrent is over quickly.

She continues to sniffle, her breathing erratic and hitching against me. It is a while before she is finally ready to look at me. Her face is blotchy, her eyes red-rimmed and her lashes soaked from her tears, and she is more beautiful than I can describe.

Tarrik offers up a kerchief that I pluck from his fingers and wipe at her tears, as the rest of the warriors gather nearby, ready to offer their support.

She takes the kerchief from me and turns and visibly begins to rebuild her defenses until she notices we have an audience.

Nola

"Oh, for fuck's sake!" I look up and not only are Truex and his brother, who looks exactly like him, I might add, staring at me, but the rest of them have also gathered around. They're trying to look busy, but it's a puny effort.

"Nola, I really want to understand why this has upset you so much." Truex drops his arms as I step away from him and try to mop up the mess my face has become, but tears flood my eyes once again. "You saw something more in your vision...about us?" he asks carefully, probably afraid he'll set me off again.

I nod and then blush. I'm not usually shy, but really? There're six of them, and we almost had sex in our dream. "When we...when we were, you know..."

"I know...?" The rascal's grin that graces his face makes me want to smack him and kiss him at the same time. I settle for wringing the damp kerchief in my fists instead of his neck.

"You threw back your head and screamed before we fell to the ground. I tried to break your fall, but you were heavy. You landed on top of me. Both of us were covered in b-blood. Don't you remember?"

"All I can recall is the pleasure of our lovemaking," he whispers to me.

"Excuse me, Nola. I am Truex's twin brother, Tarrik. You are saying that you met in his dream?"

"Yes... No. I'm a precognitive psychic. Do you know what that is?" When he shakes his head, I try to think of some other word besides charlatan that they'll understand. "What about soothsayer?"

"Ah, you see future events. You are gifted. This will be an asset to our people."

"Yes. Visions." *Really?* He thinks having visions and telling people how to find love, whether your spouse is cheating, or where to invest is an asset? And what about great disasters that no one will believe? Or the trauma of experiencing the man who's *supposed* to be your mate dying in your arms while being covered in his blood? This is what the Fae consider a gift?

"And you saw Truex injured, bleeding in your vision?" I tremble, his question mirroring my thoughts.

"Not just injured. I-I think he died." The damned tears start again, leaking down my cheeks and catching on my lips. I haven't cried this much in, well, ever.

Truex rubs a hand over my shoulder. "It will be all right." I nod, wanting so much to believe him, but I lack conviction.

"Now that we know about it, we can avoid it happening, can we not? Forewarned is forearmed, after all." A little of Tarrik's confidence seeps into my being. No. That isn't correct.

I look more closely at the brothers. I can feel their confidence vibrating in the air. Truex is pushing comfort through our connection while Tarrik is sending confidence to him, and it's spilling over and flowing into me. *Good Lord, what have I gotten myself into?*

"I don't know. The visions have never not come true."

"We will take precautions. Surely, you have been given the foresight to prevent the outcome." Tarrik nods as if his affirmative action will influence me and miraculously change the outcome of the vision.

"I didn't prevent the cataclysm. I tried to warn people, but no one would listen except for Jasmine, Tanni, and Ginger. That's why we're here. Why we survived."

"We noticed when we were in your home, you are packing?" He's an observant man. All that was sitting out were a few bags and the honey we planned to load into the car in the morning.

"Yes, we're going to try to make our way north. We're running out of supplies, and the townspeople are less than friendly. We want to leave before one of us is hurt or worse."

"We are on a mission for our prince, but if you and your friends are willing to travel with us on our mission, we will offer you all protection for the journey."

Truex has been quiet the whole time Tarrik and I have been talking. "This is okay with you?" I glance up at him shyly. What on earth is the matter with me? It's not like we're dating or something.

"Of course. It has been my intention since I learned of the possibility of you, to find you and bring you north to our home in Summer's Veil."

"I'll have to talk to the other girls. We make our decisions together but seeing as we were leaving tomorrow anyway, I don't think they will object to having an escort and extra protection. What about the other people of this town? Some of them aren't so bad, just trapped by circumstances."

"We have offered William Roberts's escort to our prince and north as far as the Lykos village of Ardiché."

I snort. "He'll be trouble. He treats the other girls like whores, even though he's afraid of me." I smile. "He thinks I'm a witch. I did curse him, after all, but he deserved it. You shouldn't trust him. No good will come from him being on this journey with us, but there are so few of us humans left, I worry the others won't follow if we leave him behind."

"Another vision?" one of the warriors asks, curiosity ripe in his voice.

"No. Just a lifelong study of human nature, and I've known him for several years."

"Will you introduce us to your lady, Truex?" another asks.

Truex grins with pride as he drops his arm over my shoulder, pulling me in close to him. I roll my eyes because he acts like he's done something wonderful. I will admit, but only to myself, his arrogance does bolster my confidence a bit.

Chapter 5

N ola
Roberts is being a freaking pain in the ass. Again. We could have left two days ago, but he's holding everyone up by lollygagging, posturing, and making ridiculous demands. If it were up to me, I would have given him an ultimatum, and when he didn't comply, I'd have left without him.

It's probably a good thing I'm not in charge, because there are other people who seem to be stuck under his authority to consider. Why they listen to him is beyond me. He's not particularly intelligent or motivated. Well, unless you consider causing discord motivation. He's always been a bit of a bully and certainly an asshole, so maybe they've misconstrued that for leadership. Who knows?

"I'm not accepting anything from any of those wh...women." Roberts hurriedly corrects himself when Truex takes a step toward him. I grab on to Truex's arm and try to pull him back toward me. It's a wasted effort because he's bigger, much stronger, and ornery. He does stop, though, saving my dignity and Roberts's face.

I huff out a breath of frustration. I'm sure everyone is feeling the same way, but Truex is ready to start ripping off vital body parts. Roberts has been taking shots at me and the girls since he found out we're going too.

I know I scared him with my prediction, and really, he should be, but there's more going on here. I get the feeling he's jealous, or he thinks with us along, he won't be able to influence the warriors. Idiot. These guys aren't going to fall for any of his bullshit. In fact, Tarrik comes across easygoing, but if you pay attention, you can see the man is a shark waiting for the chance to sink his teeth into you and pull you under.

Truex isn't any better, but you know exactly what he's thinking, and he strikes before you even know he's there. He has absolutely no tolerance for diplomacy. He's impatient and would rather strike first and ask questions later.

"If you have gas cans, and we can borrow the UTV. Truex and I will go and get enough gasoline for the journey." I've gotta do something to get Truex away from Roberts before he kills him.

Besides, I'm getting used to spending time with him, even if we are mostly surrounded by the other warriors and my friends. He's attentive, a bit of a grump, and sexy as hell. This will give us a little time alone to really talk things out.

One of the townsmen passes me the keys to the UTV while another straps gas cans onto both the bed and the back seat, while Roberts continues to glower. This thing is nicer than my first car and probably cost more too. I get in and adjust my seat and then look over at Truex. "Hop in." He's giving the vehicle a wary eye, and I can't help teasing him a little. "You're not afraid, are you? It doesn't bite."

"You do," he says, causing me to laugh. His eyes spark with a sensual glimmer. Heat rises in my cheeks. I hope no one else notices.

"I guess I do, don't I?" I answer softly.

He watches me settle myself on the seat before doing the same, and in no time, we're weaving our way through town and out into the relative openness of two countrysides from two different worlds that have melded together into one. Truex is tense at first, but as soon as there aren't any obstacles in front of us, he relaxes and seems to enjoy the experience of riding instead of walking or flying.

All too soon, we reach the driveway to the farm and turn off. It's a bumpier ride, so I slow down and concentrate on maneuvering around rubble and potholes.

"That was fun." His eyes sparkle as we come to a stop near the fuel tank and the grain bin it stands next to. "I would like to learn how to guide this beast." We both get out and start unstrapping cans.

I laugh out loud at his choice of wording. "I'll teach you how on the way back to town. How does that sound?"

He drops the cans and pulls me into his arms. "I love the sound of laughter on your lips. That I put it there makes it twice as sweet."

Oh, a silver-tongued rogue, is he? He's making it hard for me to resist him when he gets playful and flirty. One minute, he's growling, and the next, he's saying things like that. I mean, really, what's a girl supposed to do? I feel the pull between us. The humming vibration that connects us. I'm attracted to him physically. Do I take the chance and trust him? Or do I throw it away because I'm afraid?

"What has you thinking so hard, my flame?" He rubs a finger over my brow.

"You," I whisper. "You have me thinking about this, maybe taking a chance..." I wrap my arms around his neck and stare up into his jewel-blue eyes, "that this could be something real. Something good. You make me want to be crazy, to throw caution to the wind."

"Nola." He groans my name just before he captures my lips with his own. Instantly, I'm caught in the texture of his lips, the silkiness of his tongue, the excitement that flavors our breaths as we come together. My eyelids drift closed as I give myself over to the pleasure of this kiss.

Our bodies connect from chest to knee as he wraps his arms around me, lifting me closer to him. I become weightless, floating with him on a raft of desire. As my spine presses against the sun-heated metal of the grain bin, I realize he's avoided the gas cans littering the ground at our feet and has carried me into the shade of the round, squat structure.

The corrugated siding isn't comfortable, but I ignore it, placing all my attention on the man in front of me. With a few kisses, he turns my body to liquid fire and any thoughts of preservation to steam.

I want him to feel a spark of the same conflagration that's burning through me. I run my fingertips up his neck and into his sweat dampened hair. Applying pressure with my fingernails, I scratch them against his scalp before fisting my hand in his silky locks and holding him immobile as I give him my kisses.

Truex moans his pleasure and raises me higher, aligning our bodies until his cock presses against my mons. I wrap my thighs around his hips and lock my ankles against the small of his back. The little sounds that leave my lips are accompanied by a full-bodied shiver and are noises I'm sure I've never once made in my entire life.

The connection fluxing and flowing between us amplifies our emotions, spilling them between us, over and over like waves upon a seashore until I can't be certain which are mine and which are his.

I crack my eyes open as he pulls his lips from mine. The pleasure-pained grimace on his face as he tips his head back is a sight to behold. I've created that. I have power over his pleasure, just as he does mine.

Suddenly, I don't care about the outcome of that damned vision. I don't care that we've only known each other a few days. All I care about is this feeling, this passion, this connection, and that it never, ever ends.

"Put me down," I grit out. All at once, it's too much and not enough. "Truex," I beg. "Please, put me down." I drop my legs from around him. His startled *oomph* puffs against my cheek as he struggles to keep me in his arms just before my feet hit the ground.

I push against his chest, moving him an inch or so away from me. "Help me!" I beg again. Something I never thought I'd do as I begin frantically trying to get my pants undone and off my hips and legs, along with my panties. The damned things get hung up on my shoes. Tears of frustration sting my eyes, and I slap my palms against the metal siding.

"Shhh. Shhh, Nola, my flame, I have you, shhh." Truex drops to his knees at my feet and reaches for my shoelaces. I slump against the metal structure at my back. He pulls the first shoe from my foot. I can do this, I tell myself as he tugs the pants off over my foot. I can hold on one more minute, at least until I'm naked. I know I can.

Oh, how I underestimate my willpower, and I've never been so happy to be wrong in my entire life. Truex leans forward, pushing his nose into the V between my legs, and draws in a long breath through his nose and then growls. It's the sexiest thing I've ever experienced. My muscles clench. Liquid desire releases from my pussy, beckoning the predator and inviting the man kneeling at my feet to feast.

Oh, wow! Thank fuck I bathed this morning! His tongue laps at the juices dripping down my inner thighs. My breaths become jerky little pants, escalating until my head swims. I'm practically hyperventilating with the need to have his mouth fully on me.

I slip my hands into his hair and hang on. The braided ropes at his temples are tantalizing counterpoints of texture against the smooth heat of the rest of his hair. I tighten my fingers, trying to pull him closer, but he growls again and gives his head a sharp shake.

Bowing my head, I watch him nuzzle and lick my thighs. If Mr. Dominant wants to be in charge, who am I to argue? If I orgasm without him, he'll have only himself to blame.

"You will orgasm. More than once, my beauty, but only when I say so." The vibrations of his voice are so close to my clit, I squirm, involuntarily pumping my pussy toward his mouth.

"Holy shit! I said that out loud?"

"You did." Truex's pleased and sexy chuckle against my mons damn near tosses me over the edge.

I gasp and beg, gibberish leaving my lips. I'm not even sure what I'm saying. I could be speaking in tongues for all I know. "Truex," I breathe. "Please?"

He bites the edge of my fleshy lips, catching my clit between his teeth, and I'm gone. Exploding, lost, and shuddering out my release as I fly off into the cosmos.

"Nola?" His gruff whisper forces me to open eyes that I haven't realized were closed until just this moment.

"Mmmm?"

"I need to be inside you, mate. Now."

"Mmm-hmm." I agree, barely able to think, much less articulate. My legs are like cooked noodles. I'm finding it hard to stand. But a moment later, it doesn't matter. Truex power-lifts me and, using the granary against my back as leverage, cants my hips toward him. Being the helpful woman that I am, I once again wrap my legs around him.

His passion-stormed eyes meet my own. "You are mine, Nola, mine. No one else will ever have you." I nod. An agreement, my consent, whatever, this is happening because I want it to happen. I want to be his because it's my decision, kismet be damned.

He must see whatever he needs to in my eyes, because his darken as he slams himself with one thrust deep inside me.

I scream, writhing against him. The fullness of his entry and the bite of pain is a shocking revelation that soon turns to sweet, honied pleasure as he continues to thrust in and out in a frantic pounding rhythm. Little sounds leave my lips, a lilting duet to his grunts, and a beautiful accompaniment to the driving motion of his hips.

Deep within me, I can feel my muscles tighten as the walls of my sex begin to flutter. Truex thrusts harder, and just like he promised he would, he launches my body into another orgasm. But this time, I don't fly alone. He joins me as universes collide and stars crash together, and we fall in sparkling flashes of mutual pleasure.

"Truex, tell me about your species. We've been intimate, but I hardly know anything about you other than you're Fae. On Earth, the Fae are just myths. Our stories are rarely complimentary to your species unless it's a steamy romance. You would fit perfectly in one of those," I tease. I lie next to him, amazed by his sweetness. He's grumpy with everyone else, but a marshmallow with me. He's created a bed of soft magic and flower petals to cushion our bodies and keep us out of the dirt. I lie on my back, staring up into the crisp blueness of the midday sky as Truex stretches out on his side, facing me.

"We Fae are an ancient species. We've been around as long if not longer than the Infernion, the Caélumi, and the Lykosians. Our home world is called Elfame, and Summer's Veil is an outpost here in Tellus."

"So, your species doesn't normally live here either?"

"We do...or we did." Sadness washes over his features. "Our queen presided over the Enlightened City, Atlantaes. It was a bright and glowing jewel in the middle of a sparkling sea, filled with knowledge and magic, where beings from all the realms, including Earth, could pass through the Omnichronos to come and learn from us."

"Atlantis? Holy shit! That's incredible. Jasmine's not going to believe this. What's the Omnichronos?"

"The Omnichronos is what made realm travel possible. It was the seat of wild magic and immense power. It held the balance of all the realms. It's gone now along with our queen and there is very little chance we will ever return to Elfame." He contemplatively brushes a blade of grass along the contours of my still naked body, tickling me and causing the flesh to pebble. "But finding you has given my brethren hope that each of us will find the mate destiny has chosen for all of us, so all is not lost."

"And the Infernion, Caélumi, and Lykosians? I think I've seen them in visions. Who are they?" I shiver, brushing away the itching sensation his ministrations have caused.

"The Infernion are loud, crazy barbarians, a dragon species. They wield fire and brimstone and have an affinity for all that is terra firma, including earthquakes and volcanos. They are smart and usually up to no good." His mouth brushes against the sensitive area between my shoulder and collarbone as he speaks.

"Hmm, kind of like you, huh?"

"Exactly like me." I feel his lips stretch in a smile against my skin before he continues answering my questions.

"The Caélumi are winged beings who believe they are the superior race. They are arrogant and cold. Their magic is connected to the sky, storms, wind, and lightning. They tend to bluster just like thunder, and about as effectively too." Truex's snort of disdain tells me he's hardly impressed.

"The Lykos are shapeshifters. They don't become animals, but they can and do take on animal like characteristics. They can increase in size. They are excellent hunters, trackers, and can fight with the best of us even without spells or sigils at their disposal. They are also the most hierarchical beings among us. They live in packs with an alpha as a ruler over each. There is a constant fight to be top dog, so to speak."

"Why do you think that is?"

He shrugs. "It is their nature."

"It's strange that I've seen all these species in visions, but only males."

"That is because the Lykos and humans are the only ones who have any females left. The rest of the species, Fae included, have been slowly fading away by attrition. No females means no mates. No mates means no children. Never has a child been born to us without the mating connection. Our prince has heard and felt his mate here in Tellus, so we came to search for her, and lo and behold, I have found you. You, Nola, represent hope for me and my brethren. For our entire species. You are a miracle. You are my everything, and I will cherish you as such for as long as we both shall live."

"Hmm." The reverence I hear in his tone shortens my breath. The connection flowing between us is strong, I'm afraid of how quickly things have happened, but I'm also excited. I've never been anyone's *everything* before. It's thrilling and exhilarating and, frankly, scary as hell.

"Do not fear what is between us, Nola," he whispers. "It is strong and true and will become more comfortable with time." He pulls me close, turning me to him as he captures my lips with his own, and my fears disappear, at least temporarily, beneath the magic of our renewed passion.

It was late when we got back to town, and of course, Roberts raised holy hell, erasing some of the joy and contentment an afternoon spent in Truex's arms created. Some, but not all.

Roberts is blaming us for getting a late start this morning, when it was obvious he was the one holding us up. Everyone else had been ready to go for an hour. Once again, I had to persuade Truex not to murder him when Roberts's comments turned vulgar. He's going to make one too many references to what we must have been doing to be gone for so long and how it wasn't appropriate behavior on my part, and Truex will take his head off.

"How far do you think we'll go today?" Jasmine asks from beside me as we bump over the potholed and cracked surface of what was once a state highway mixed with the terrain of this new realm we're in.

"I'm not certain. Roberts is acting like he's the expedition leader. I'm surprised Tarrik or Truex haven't dumped him in a hole by now. I guess we'll stop when we stop." I watch as the warriors in the form of crows fly ahead and then circle back, with Truex occasionally coming to fly by my window. What would it be like to be so free?

"Man, I've got to pee so bad," Jasmine grumbles.

"Same."

"Me too."

Ginger and Tanni chime in, and I laugh because I could use a bathroom break and a stretch of my legs too. Even though we're riding in a Caddy and have plenty of leg room, none of us are used to sitting in one spot for so long. We're not used to being in a car at all.

Up ahead, I see a long, squat building and make a split-second decision to leave our convoy. Slowing a bit, I take the driveway faster than I probably should, since the car bounces over the ruts and rubble.

"Nola! What the hell? Do you want me to piss in the car?" Jasmine yells. The other girls groan, probably from the abuse to their bladders, but then giggle when we finally rock to a stop in front of a worn but still intact roadhouse.

I grin as I push open my door, happy to stand and stretch, but pause midmotion when the door of the bar swings open and a scary-looking group of leather-wearing bikers step out onto the porch.

"Uh-oh," Jasmine whispers.

Before anyone can say anything, Truex shifts as he lands in front of me. Ronan and then Rylan shift following right after. Glancing toward our convoy, I see the trucks have stopped and the rest of the warriors look like black bullets racing through the sky, growing bigger and bigger as they get nearer to us.

I feel like I need to defuse the situation before it escalates.

"Um, hi." I lean to the side so I can peek around Truex and wave my hand. "We just wanted to stop to use a bathroom and stretch our legs. We prefer not to cause any trouble."

"...and Lord, do I have to use the bathroom!" Ginger sings out, her voice warbling and high-pitched. Tanni starts to giggle, and the stern faces of the bikers crack into reluctant grins, but then sober again as the rest of the warriors land.

Soon after, Roberts comes tearing into the driveway, sending gravel and dirt flying as he skids to a stop. Emma, who, by the way, is riding in the bed of the truck, almost tumbles out.

He jumps from his vehicle and starts shouting as he storms toward me. "You are not in charge here, witch!"

"Neither are you, asshole!" Jasmine, who has come to my side, puts herself between us as Truex grabs my arm, pulling me back.

The crack of Roberts's hand hitting Jasmine's cheek and her subsequent cry of surprised pain is almost as loud as the sound of a shotgun being racked. Everyone who isn't Fae freezes until a voice calls out from the porch. The warriors are already in motion, pushing Roberts away as Rylan steps in front of Jasmine.

"Son, you lay your hand on a woman in anger again in my presence and see what happens." A grizzled older man looks like your stereotypical biker, with a bandana on his head, long salt-and-pepper beard, leather vest and chaps, and a scowl on his face that gives nothing away. He isn't the one holding the shotgun, but it's plain to see he's the man in charge.

Roberts, showing some common sense for once, reluctantly backs away. He meets my gaze, and I narrow my eyes, giving him my nastiest look. He flinches before turning around and getting back into his truck. If it weren't for Emma, the run-down young woman he calls his wife, I would suggest leaving him behind, but every life is valuable, if not essential. Hopefully, he'll pull his head out of his ass and realize he needs the rest of us more than we need him.

"My name's Beach. You're welcome here. Does anyone else have to use the bathroom besides the redhead?" the old biker asks. Tanni, Jasmine, and I all raise our hands and so does Roberts's wife. "Well, come on with you. Then we'll getcha squared away. We don't have a lot by the way of food, but we can share what we have."

Tarrik steps forward to offer a handshake in the human way, something Tanni and Ginger taught the Fae, along with a warrior's greeting of grasping the forearm.

"We thank you for your hospitality."

Beach must be used to manly displays, because he doesn't bat an eye at the extra form of greeting. I'm going to have to try to explain human weapons to the warriors. Every one of them is seriously underestimating the human capacity for cruelty and the urge to shoot first and ask questions later, especially in this new realm.

Beach turns to one of the men next to him after all the greetings are exchanged among the males. "James, go help that little lady down from the bed of that truck." Beach's man hurries to comply as a couple of men behind him grunt and nod. It's obvious he's a man of authority and his people respect him.

"We have food, sir. We'd be happy to share, after we use the facilities, of course," I offer in return for their hospitality.

Chapter 6

T ruex

Beach and his followers agreed to travel with us after hearing where we were headed. Their supplies were becoming dangerously low, and they would have to leave their home anyway. It made sense to leave with us as a larger group would afford both parties better security. They had bartered with a few small groups on their way north that had seen the Infernion and had horror stories to tell. Tarrik snorted at the retellings, indicating they are tall tales, so I'm reserving judgement. It appears the Humans are allowing their fears and imaginations to run wild.

I like Beach and his followers much better than Roberts and some of his. He seems the trustworthy sort. When we left this morning, Roberts was not pleased to be ordered to *allow* the bikers to ride at the front of the line. Beach did not care. I thought for a moment the two men would come to blows, but Roberts backed down when Beach's men backed him up. That Beach has the loyalty of his men and women says much about the man. He will make a good ally, and perhaps even better friend. Time will tell.

As we approached the outskirts of a larger melded and broken city, travel became more difficult for both the bikers and the vehicles. As it was coming up on dusk, we decided it was better to enter the city in daylight, so we made camp.

Just past the witching hour, Carson and Ronan, the warriors on watch, witnessed the might of our prince's magic, explosions of noise, flame, and destruction on the other side of the city. What they did not hear or see was magic from any of our brethren in the elite guard. That our prince may be fighting alone has us all on edge.

For once in my life, I am divided in my duty. Do I go to the aid of my prince, or do I stay and guard the woman who is the other half of my soul? Tarrik, knowing my anxiety, orders me to stay with the humans, but I am torn.

"Truex, think of Nola's vision," he reminds me. "The fire, lightning, and explosions could be what she saw. I will not risk you, brother. Stay and watch over the humans. I will leave Rylan with you."

"But Tarrik..."

"No. I am third in command. This is an order from your commander," he snaps. That he would order me is telling. He worries about the vision coming to pass more than he has let on.

Soon after, he, Carson, Ronan, and Basil leave to go to the aid of the prince, while Rylan and I patrol the perimeter of the camp. I am still torn between wishing I was with them and happy I was left behind.

"Everything okay?" Nola's voice in the darkness startles me.

"Our prince is distressed. Most of the others have gone to his aid."

"Why did you stay behind? You're the muscle, the enforcer, aren't you?"

"The muscle?" Even under the stress of this untenable situation, she makes me smile.

"You know what I mean." She playfully pinches my side as I pull her into my arms.

"Yes, I am the enforcer, but Tarrik thought it would be best if I stayed behind this time. Perhaps he thought my concentration would be divided between my prince's safety and your own."

"Or he's worried that my vision would come to pass."

"That too. You are perceptive."

"I can feel your emotions, and through you, some of his. Probably because he's your twin." She shrugs and settles more closely against me. "The vibration isn't as strong, but it's there."

"I am not certain that I like that you are able to feel Tarrik, but I know he would like it even less than I."

"Believe me, I'm not thrilled about it either. I was getting some decent sleep until you two started worrying and stirring up my emotions. I'm just starting to wrap my head around the two of us sharing a link, adding a third to the mix is a little unsettling."

"As long as it is *only* emotion through the link that is added as a third..." I sound like a jealous idiot. "You should try to get some more sleep. I have a feeling tomorrow is going to be a rough day."

"No worries, big guy. There will be no thirds for either of us, brother or not."
She rises on her toes and kisses the corner of my mouth before pulling out of
my arms and heading back to her bedroll.

We are pushing the humans hard, but the urgency to find our prince is pressing
upon us. Tarrik and the others arrived too late. Our prince was gone in a trail of
destruction leading out onto the Waste. An angry group of humans scrambled
to organize themselves. It seems they had been caught unaware. Tarrik left
those humans to their own devices when he realized they were armed the same
as Beach and his men. After Nola informed us of what the human weapons
could do, James gave us a small presentation with bottles set out on a fence.
Assuming that these were the people assailing our prince, but not knowing for
sure, he left them unharmed.

Weaving our way around the outskirts of the city took hours. Tarrik finally
agreed to again stop for the night when it became too dangerous for the
vehicles to pass safely through the rubble in the growing darkness.

With the first light of dawn breaking over the horizon, we are on our way
again, this time out onto the flats of the Waste, and waste it is. It is a flat brown
desert like terrain dotted with the remnants of stone buildings, now just ruins.
This was ground zero, where the realms collided in the cataclysm. Nothing of
substance remains. It feels like we are flying over a burial site. In essence, we
are, for no one survived from Tellus or Earth this far in.

Rylan, who is flying point, cries out first as a crow and then as a warrior as
he races back to the convoy. "There is smoke in the distance!"

Tarrik signals to the convoy, and we roll to a stop. He quickly determines that
Rylan, Basil, and Ronan will go forward to provide reconnaissance, but before
our warriors can depart, two black specks fly toward us.

It isn't long before two more Fae elite guards, Payne and Marril, change
and greet us. I stand quietly as we get news that our prince is safe, and Tarrik
fills Payne in on the high points of our journey. Payne then takes to the air,
racing back to our prince's camp, while Marril stays to help get the convoy
moving again. I think he is curious about the humans we have with us. He will

be surprised to find I am mated, but I choose not to share that information until after I introduce her to my prince.

Nola

I'm not sure what I expected a royal prince to look like, but it certainly isn't the man waiting for the convoy. His hair looks like multifaceted crystals blowing in the breeze. I can't make out his eye color, but he's just as big and muscular as Truex.

"Holy shit! That's the prince?" Ginger whistles under her breath.

I'm kind of feeling the same way, but it isn't the prince who's caught my attention. It's the woman at his side. They're a stunning couple, even dirty and dressed like soldiers. Her ash-blonde hair is severely pulled back from her face in a tight braid, and her skin is flawless. It's the way she stands, the way she holds herself, like she's the commander of an army, that gives me pause. She isn't much younger than I am, but it's plain to see, this is a woman who has been to war and come out the other side victorious.

Her eyes are sharp and assessing; she is judge, jury, and executioner all rolled into one, and it makes me nervous. Will she turn us away? Find the girls and I are somehow lacking or unacceptable? It's been so long that I cared what other people thought about me that I've forgotten what this debilitating doubt of myself feels like, and I can't say as I like revisiting it.

"Well, it's now or never." I notice the rest of our group getting out of their vehicles. I look at Jasmine. She's feeling the same way, but we nod and push our doors open at the same time.

Truex arrives at my side, helping me from the car. He then lays my hand formally in the crook of his elbow and escorts me toward his prince. I pause for a moment, looking back at my girls before waving for them to follow.

Roberts reaches the prince just before we do. I'm tickled when the prince ignores him completely and instead places the woman's hand on his arm and introduces her as the Lady Raven, his consort, to the Fae warriors gathering around him.

Roberts, the dumbass, has the audacity to interrupt and introduce himself.

"Will the rest of your people be joining you, William Roberts?" the prince asks.

"No. They know their place. As I was telling your man, it's important that we humans establish a seat of power here. You'll do well to throw in with us. It would be to your advantage."

I can't help it; a small snort leaves my lips. That Roberts thinks he has any bargaining power or advantage here is laughable.

The Lady Raven must think so too, because she calls a warrior forward and sends him to gather the others who came with us, all the while staring down William Roberts.

When he begins to protest, she refers to the movie *The Wizard of Oz* and basically tells him to shut it because he isn't in Kansas anymore.

The girl has balls! I want to cheer. It isn't until later that we discover just how much authority this woman carries, though, and the lengths she'll go to protect those under her care.

Roberts is once again being a loudmouthed prick and offers up some of us *less acceptable women* to appease the slavers. His eyes land on me briefly before snapping to Raven. I expect the prince to rip him a new one, but Raven handles him beautifully, putting him in his place and reassuring the rest of us.

Before anyone can suggest that he sit down and shut up, he hammers the final nail into his proverbial coffin.

"Whoo-wee." His attention is caught by someone behind the prince. Everyone turns to look, except for Raven and the prince. Roberts makes them an offer.

"How about a trade? My wife, she's a worker... For that set of twins." The dumbass licks his lips, and the Lady Raven loses her shit. She's moving faster than I've ever seen a human move! She's across the circle, knife drawn and stabbing it into Roberts almost faster than anyone can comprehend. They go down in a flurry of arms and legs with Roberts squealing like a stuck pig.

The prince wades in and pulls Raven off Roberts.

Roberts spews profanities as his cronies lift him from the ground.

"You bitch!" Roberts screams. "Fucking whore, I'm gonna kill you!"

"Try it, motherfucker! I see you look at one of *my* kids again, and you're a dead man! I didn't save each of them from the slavers only to turn them over to the likes of you!" Held securely within the prince's arms, she adds the final blow. "You're done here. Get in your shit vehicle and go! You've used up your first and last chance with us."

She glares at the rest of us, and it's then that I notice her witchy two-colored eyes. "If the rest of you feel the same as him, you're gone too." This incredible woman, this Amazon warrior, is scary as hell. A ping of intuition tells me that she's the one in charge, but the rest of them haven't figured it out yet, even her prince, and I hope I'm around to watch how this unfolds.

"Bitch, you have no say..." A spark of blue magic lands on Roberts's lips, sealing them together and locking his words inside.

I stand there, awed. I know Truex can do spells and magic, but with a flick of his fingers, the prince just sealed someone's lips shut? Holy fuck! We most definitely are not in Kansas!

During the early morning hours before dawn, I was surprised to see Raven up and patrolling the camp. She's nothing like I thought she would be. She's friendly, funny, serious, and rock steady. We share a cup of coffee and bond over our mutual circumstance of being destined mates.

This is the first morning I haven't had to deal with Roberts and his dirty looks. Frankly, it's a load off my shoulders I didn't realize I was carrying until he was sent on his way yesterday.

Afterward, I decided to go back to bed in hopes of getting another hour of sleep, but there's something niggling at the edge of my awareness, not allowing me to rest.

Like so many times, when I can't get my mind to settle, I reach for my tarot cards. Shuffling them has a calming effect. It helps me disassociate from whatever is bothering me and allows my subconscious to work through the problem. I shuffle for nearly five minutes, enjoying the sound of the cards sliding and flicking against one another. Just as I'm about to put them away, a bunch of cards flip from between my nimble fingers and fall. Thunder rumbles in the distance, rolling across the barren landscape.

"Wha... Was that thunder?" Jasmine asks. Her voice is heavy with sleep and confusion. We haven't had a thunderstorm or any rain at all to speak of in months.

"Yeah." I glance down at the wayward cards, my hand stalling in midmovement to gather them. Laying before me is the sixteenth and seventeenth cards of the Major Arcana, the Tower and the Star, along with the Two of Cups from the Minor Arcana.

Lightning smashes into the tower, causing devastation and toppling the spire. A naked man falls seemingly to his death. Chills run down my spine as thunder sounds across the Waste again. If the Tower were right-side up, I'd be shitting bricks, but the card is inverted.

Ah-ha! This is the unsettled feeling I haven't been able to put my finger on. Whoever is represented as the Star is about to be toppled, for this card too is inverted. There's no doubt whatever is coming is going to suck, faith will be tested, and hope lost. But the third card tells me that if the couple sharing their magic will hang on and trust, the situation will right itself and everything will turn out okay.

But who is this couple? Is it Truex and me? Is my earlier vision coming to pass? Is it Raven and the prince? Will anyone believe me if I say something? What if I don't, and I could change the way things happen? What am I going to do?

I don't get the chance to figure it out because agitated shouts ring out through the camp, calling everyone to the prince's fire.

"Oh, shit! Oh, shit! Oh, shit!" I chant as I pull on my shoes and jump to my feet. "Hurry!"

Jasmine and the other girls scramble to get their shoes on, and we race toward the fire near the huge military truck and the prince's fire.

"What's going on?" Tanni asks.

"I don't know, but nothing good."

As we approach the growing crowd, I search for Truex, finding him and Tarrik standing, heads bent together, sharing an intense conversation. I rush to him, relief flashes in his eyes as he pulls me into his arms and captures my lips the way he kissed me the first time in the vision.

"No!" I yank myself away, frantically looking behind him.

"Nola, by the Lady, what are you doing?" He's confused by my pulling away, but right now, I don't care. I'm desperate in my need to protect him.

"Nola!" Tarrik snaps.

"Tarrik…" The not-so-subtle warning in Truex's voice as he practically growls his brother's name tugs my attention back to the brothers.

"No. Nola, what is it? Do you know something?" Tarrik stares down at me in intense concentration. "Tell me."

"I don't know, the kiss…it was similar to the dream…but the rest, I just don't know…and then the cards." I grab Truex's hand, clinging to him, needing the connection.

The need to keep him safe and near bubbles up within me, volcanic and pressing to make it so. He's a grown man. A powerful and magical Fae warrior, but he won't be able to protect himself from the coming nightmare I saw in the vision. Grief, so overwhelming, so strong at the thought of his loss assails me. How did this happen so quickly? I need this man! I am so in over my head. I don't know what to do. I can't think straight.

Truex pulls me with him, protecting his back by placing it against the door of the military-style truck and tucking me into his arms.

"Nola, focus. Can you do that?" The calm seriousness of Tarrik's voice allows me to pull back from the full-blown panic taking over. "This is not the same situation as the vision?"

"N-no." I think back to the vision. "The intensity of this kiss was the same as that first kiss and the thunder rumbling, but the rest is different."

"Then what spooked you? Was it the cards?"

"Yes. They tell a story of destruction, lost hope, and confusion, but I can't say if it's for us, or for someone else." I grip the arm Truex is holding me with, finding comfort in his warm embrace.

We're interrupted when first Raven and then Orion march with purposeful strides into the middle of the group. Intuition whispers to me, and it's then I know the cards aren't meant for Truex and me, but for Raven and Orion. They have a rough road to follow in the very near future.

Chapter 7

T ruex

"I have never put children to bed before. Are they usually so rambunctious and needy?" I ask as Nola shifts in my arms as she sits between my legs in front of the campfire.

It's been two days since Orion and Raven returned from their mission to rescue seven more children from a battle between the Caélumi and the Infernion. We now have fourteen children in camp between the ages of one and eighteen, half of them under the age of ten.

We have reached the Lykosian city of Ardiché, and Raven and Orion have gone into the city to parley with the alphas to see if they want to take in the Lykosian children within our care.

"I've never been around kids either. How did your prince talk us into watching them? I don't know how Raven does it."

"I am baffled as well. She does it so effortlessly, and they listen to her."

Raven looked worn and subdued when they returned. She was reluctant to let Orion out of her sight. According to Payne, they thought they had lost Orion for more than a few minutes, and she was devastated, but didn't let it show. She soldiered on, stood her ground when many would have folded. Payne's and Keller's estimation of her has grown. They, along with the human, James, now call her My Lady, treating her with the deference due a queen. That she is human does not bother Payne in the least. She has gained his loyalty and his devotion.

"She probably scares them into submission," Nola jokes, and I laugh.

"She has their trust and loyalty, even more so than some of the warriors who are already falling under her spell."

"What do you mean, spell?" The fire crackles and pops as I try to put into words what I am thinking.

"Having sway over people is a type of magic. Influence is a powerful tool, a weapon in the wrong hands, a blessing in the right ones. Raven has that. Her personal magic is strong, and I worry about the wellbeing of my prince."

"This bothers you, Truex? If they're mates, and it seems they are, it's good she can handle herself, especially if destiny has paired her with a prince, also a person of influence."

"It is unsettling to me that she seems to pull people in so quickly. It is suspicious that it is happening so fast among the warriors. Especially Payne."

"I think Raven's allure for the others is because she's fiercely independent. She's scared, but not once does she back down, even in the face of danger or opposition. She's also kind. These kids, every single one of them, have been rescued by her, cared for by her, and protected by her. They know they can depend on her. She treats them as members of her family. I think your warriors are beginning to see the same thing, and it is something they want for themselves."

Raven didn't hesitate to try to kill Roberts when he disrespected the twin girls, or to take in Emma, the pregnant, cast-off woman Roberts had claimed as a wife until he saw something he wanted more. Nola is good at reading people. She has survived from doing so; therefore, maybe what she says is true. I will have to think on it.

"Perhaps," I allow. "Time will tell. Until then, I will hold my judgment or reverence and wait for proof." I rest my fingers beneath her chin, tilting it just so, holding my lips just above her own. "You have already earned my regard and a reward."

"A reward, huh? For what?" Her lips brush against mine, a sensual and beguiling tease of sensitive flesh barely touching sensitive flesh.

"For." *Kiss.* "Just." *Kiss.* "Being." *Kiss.* "You." I punctuate each word with a little smacking kiss before taking her mouth on a surge of growing excitement. That is, until someone clears their throat.

"Umm, Mr. Truex, sir?" A bashful voice on the perimeter of the firelight interrupts us.

Nola bursts into laughter before mumbling something about Raven and her birth control measures. I have no idea what she is talking about, so I ignore it for now and concentrate on the nervous woman-child in front of us.

"Annalise? What is it?"

"Ummm, well, you see... Emma and I both have to use the...facilities?"

"Facilities?" I am completely confused. Nola again laughs, but sheds light on the problem at hand.

"The girls have to take a piss, and you and Tarrik warned them not to go anywhere alone. Am I right, Annalise?"

"Yes, ma'am." A nervous titter follows, and Emma, who has stayed behind her, offers a timid smile.

"I thought as much. I shall make use of the *facilities* too. Come, Truex, you may escort us ladies to the potty." Nola affects a funny accent, causing all three women to burst into a fit of giggles.

Sighing at the interruption and silly feminine humor, I get to my feet and pull Nola to hers. Why they didn't just say privy and why they seem to be embarrassed about doing a normal bodily function, I don't know. Females are both confusing and delightful in an *I have no idea why I am doing this* kind of way.

If it makes Nola laugh with such joy, I will be happy to escort her to the moon if she so wishes it. I will not tell her this because she would then most certainly ask me to prove it, and I would, of course, do my best to make it so.

Nola

"Well, that was embarrassing," Annalise grouses. "At least it wasn't Zek..." The blush on her pretty cheeks makes me smile.

"Somebody's got a cru-ush!" I singsong, making Emma snicker. It's the first sound I've heard from her since Roberts left. Annalise's face turns even redder. It's obvious she has her eye on one of the elite guards that's been protecting the prince.

"I'm not the only one crushing on a hottie! I saw you sucking face with Truex by the fire. Why don't you do your business first and then go back to smooching on your man?"

"Oh-ho! You know what? That's a good idea!" I do what needs to be done and snag a baby wipe from the package to clean my hands.

Feeling lighter than I have in forever, I playfully skip back to Truex, throwing myself into his arms when I reach him.

"It is a good thing we do not have to be stealthy and quiet. You ladies are making enough noise for the whole camp. People are trying to sleep, you know?"

"Always such a grump, aren't you?" I tease.

"I do not know what a hottie is, but when my *smooching* is interrupted, I do tend to get a little surly."

I smile. Maybe we were being a bit loud, but we've been under so much strain, it feels good to laugh and make new friends without the stigma of my old life weighing me down.

"Well, we can pick up where we left off." I blow him an air kiss just to see what he'll do.

"Indeed, we can." His eyes turn bright with passion, gleaming with seduction in the light of the fairy lanterns placed along the path to the temporary outdoor toilets.

I feel as if I'm falling, caught in his magnetic presence. His beautiful possessive eyes, his delicious scent, that gorgeous, sculpted mouth. I place my hand over his heart, licking my lips as his fingertips brush my collarbone and shivers race over my body. His hand drifts over my shoulder before grasping a fistful of my braids.

I pant in excitement as he tips my head, guiding my lips to his own. I rise onto my tiptoes, clutching at him, digging my fingernails into his flesh through his shirt. His sensual growl heightens my arousal, and I moan in response.

Our mouths come together, passion exploding between us. His other hand wraps around my back, pulling me more tightly against him until I can feel his sex pressing into my stomach. I lift my leg, twinging myself around him.

Lightning flashes bright and shattering against my eyelids, and I frown, my concentration on Truex disrupted. Thunder rumbles much closer than expected.

I feel more than hear Truex growl as he pulls his lips from mine and bends me backward. He pushes my blouse aside and sinks his teeth into my skin before sucking hard.

Sinking my hands into his hair, I wrestle to clear my head from the lust-induced fog he's created around us. Lightning flashes again much closer and more disorienting as thunder hammers right on top of us.

Truex throws back his head, screaming as he takes us to the ground. My head hits the hard-packed dirt with stunning force as his body lands on top of me. I have a moment when a flare of pain forces me to cognizance, but all too soon, I'm lost again to the wooziness in my head and the horror of the hot viscosity of Truex's blood flowing over me. I open my mouth to scream, but another blow lands against my cheek, and I melt into darkness.

Panic, jagged and hot, rips through me when I can't open my eyes. The jostling movement beneath me makes me dizzy and nauseous. I vomit, choking, and gasping for air. I try to roll to my side, crying out as pain, jagged and tearing, rips through my injured body.

"Stupid bitch!"

The kick that lands near my hip has me gagging, and I battle not to puke again. The pounding in my head escalates as I waver between staying awake and fading into unconsciousness.

Small, strong hands roll me to my side while tugging me away from the mess I've created. A sharp staccato of blows rains down on something metal nearby, and I breathe a silent but thankful sigh of relief as whatever is moving beneath me slows and then rocks to a stop.

An irritated voice shouts, "What?"

"The fuckin' stupid bitch puked all over back here, man. I ain't riding in it! These bitches aren't going anywhere. Hell if I'm smelling that the rest of the way!" The leaf springs rock as the man gets out of the bed of the truck, making it bounce and sway, and I almost throw up again as I groan in agony.

Soon after, doors slam and the truck is moving, shuddering, and bumping over the rough terrain. *What the hell is goin' on?*

"Shh. Nola, shh. You'll be all right. Raven will come for us. I know she will. Raven will come."

"Annalise?" A particularly rough bump has us flying into the air and slamming back into the bed. I moan as my head connects with what must be someone's knee. I can't see to get my bearings. It's then that I realize it's not just Annalise and me being tossed around back here.

"Yeah, me and Emma. We're okay, well, Emma's face is turning the color of an eggplant, and she's having trouble talking because it hurts, but apart from that, we're okay for now. It's you we've been worried about. You're covered in b-blood!" The sob that breaks free at the end wrenches my heart.

"What happened?"

"Y-you don't remember?"

"No."

"There were all kinds of explosions. We started to run back to camp, but Emma was grabbed, and I stayed to help her. They threw us back here and pointed guns at us, and then they came running with you and threw you in! I didn't see Truex, but I know Raven will come, I know she will. She found me the first time. She'll find us again...we just have to h-hold on."

"Tru...ex?" Oh, God! The vision of Truex screaming and us being covered in blood is true. It's all come true. He's dead. A shattered wail pushes past my lips. I barely had time to know him, love him, cherish him, and now he's gone.

"He's gone. He's gone."

"Nola, no! You don't know that! You don't! Raven will make everything all right, you'll see! Please, Nola, please! You don't know that!"

"I do know! I saw it! Weeks ago, I saw it! And I feel it now! He's gone!" As my volume increases, the pounding in my head escalates, bludgeoning me with every heartbeat, every labored breath. I lay panting, sobbing out my misery as I stare into the puddle of my vomit. Will we survive this new hell we've been cast into? Another, even more painful thought nags at me through the pain—do I even want to?

I don't know if it's the head injury, the pain racking my body, or the loss of Truex, but I sink into a hellish stupor on a never-ending ride to hell. I surface when we hit rough patches, but most of the time, I drift in and out of consciousness, wishing that I could fall asleep and wake up in Truex's arms and this nightmare would only be a dream.

The slamming of the truck's doors barely registers until the tailgate is dropped with a heavy, metallic thunk.

My ankles are grabbed and pulled, and feeble as I am, I kick out, catching someone.

"God dammit!" a pissed-off voice growls before I'm yanked out of the bed of the truck.

I'm weightless for probably a little less than a second before my arm and then head bounce off the ground with my feet still suspended in the air. When my full weight hits, the snapping of my forearm beneath my body is as loud as a gunshot. And even with the breath knocked out of me, I twist and puke again. My head explodes as the pain is amplified so much so, that I again start to sink into unconsciousness.

"Roberts, you're a fucking dumbass. Stop damaging the merchandise!" a distant voice scolds. "Get them cleaned up and set up the tent. We'll camp here. There's no one on the back trail, so it'll be safe enough."

I'm dragged on my knees through the dirt, and although Annalise tries to help by getting under my arm and lifting me to my feet, it just hurts worse.

"It's broken," I tell her as I tuck my arm close to my body.

"I know. I heard it."

Roberts pushes me to the ground, and Annalise sprawls with me as I fall. This time, when I meet dirt, it's also against a rough stone structure. At least it's in some shade, I can feel the difference in temperature immediately.

I hear something slosh. I gasp as wetness touches my face.

"It's okay. They gave us some water. I'm just wiping the dried blood from your face. There we go." Annalise gently lays the cloth in my good hand. Try to wipe some blood off your lashes. I don't want to hurt you."

"Where's Emma?" I dab at my eyes, but the blood is so dried and crusted, I need to scrub at it.

"She's here. Roberts hit her again. I'm so scared, Nola. They're watching me; It makes me feel sick." Her voice wobbles.

Annalise is trying to be brave, but really, she's just a kid, maybe fifteen or sixteen years old. She's tiny too, probably an inch or so over five feet tall, curvy, stacked, and cute as can be.

I finally remove enough blood from my left eye so I can crack it open. "We stick together, you two hear me? We fight, we lie, we kill if we must. Understand?"

My vision is blurry, and the light causes a piecing pain. I blink a couple of times before switching to a clean spot on the cloth and starting on the other eye.

"We could lie and say you're more hurt than you are, that you need us to help you and watch over you because you have a concussion." Annalise sounds so hopeful, rallying now that she has a mission.

"Yeah, but it's not a lie. I do have a concussion, and this wrist is going to need to be set." I hold my swollen wrist up, cringing when it throbs. "It's not gonna be pretty or fun, but it needs to be done."

Emma bumps into both Annalise and me, jarring my arm but making us aware that someone is approaching. I gag just as Roberts walks back to us. I squint up at him. He blanches when he sees I'm watching him. It gives me satisfaction to know that even battered and bloody, he's still afraid of me. I'll use that information to my advantage if I can.

"Not so high and mighty now, are you?" The skeevy look he casts toward Annalise makes my skin crawl. Emma, bless her soul, draws his attention away from the girl. Even though her jaw is almost black with bruising and must pain her, she speaks, putting herself in the crosshairs of Roberts's anger.

"Nola neebs gare. 'Er arm an 'er 'ead."

"Shut up, bitch. You sound stupid. I'll hit you again, and you won't be talking at all." He swings his gaze back to Annalise. "Come on, girl. The boys and I got a surprise for you."

"You remember what I told you, Roberts? It's still coming for you." I slowly stand, with Annalise's help. "She's staying right here. I need her to set my arm."

"She has a h-head injury too. The others aren't going to be happy if she dies," Annalise adds. Her voice is shaky, but she holds her ground.

Roberts looks like he's about to explode, but then looks back toward the main hub of the camp. "You just wait. Your time is coming. Before we sell you off to the monsters, I'ma make sure I shove my cock in you." Spit flies from his mouth as he viciously points his finger at Annalise's face. I subtly move until my body is half blocking hers from his view.

"With your every word, your end is coming nearer and nearer, Roberts. I can feel it just around the corner." I let my eyes go soft focused as if I'm seeing his death happening. I let a small smile play on my lips, hoping it looks serene, knowing.

"The boys are setting up a tent. You get your asses in there and stay quiet, or so help me, you'll regret the consequences." He storms away and sends over the two men who followed him out of our camp.

They both avoid my eyes, but I see them looking at Annalise. She's practically pushed up against my back, trying to hide, by the time they're done setting up the tent. One of them hands Emma a small pack before they finally motion to go in.

Even though it's going to be stifling, it's a relief to be out from under their scrutiny and evil looks.

"Let's get this over with and then we've got to make a plan and get the hell away from them." I motion to the floor, and they help me lie down. "Okay, here's what I need you to do." I give them details of how to set my wrist. The first pull of realigning movement and the sound of bones grating together coalesces into a vortex of agony that shoves me into the blissful well of nothingness.

Chapter 8

Despite Annalise and Emma's attempt to splint my arm, the pain is getting worse, especially with the continued shaking of my body. Tears leak from between my eyelids, dripping from my nose and running into my ear as I lie here in the darkness. I've been awake on and off throughout the night, unable to rest properly.

The fever and chills started hours ago. I awaken, shaking physically and mentally, not sure why, until I hear Annalise's animal-like grunts of fear and torment. I lunge to my feet, gasping. Staggering from the tent, I push past physical discomfort, frantically looking for the girl. I'll do what I can to protect her.

"Annalise? Annalise!" My hoarse shouts draw our captors' attention. A few come running toward me. The noise she's making is suddenly muffled. Fear settles sharp and cold in my stomach. "Where is she?" I snarl, ready to kill every single one of them with my bare hands.

Three men and a woman stop in front of me. "Goddamn it, motherfucker, where is she?" I demand.

"Who?"

Who? "Annalise, you cocksucker! I can hear her crying! Where is she? I'm gonna curse you and every single one of your men if a hair on that girl's head is mussed! Your testicles are gonna shrivel and fall off, see if they won't! Your cocks will look like Grinch ornaments, diseased and putrid! Your..."

"Bitch! Shut up! Where's Roberts?" Just as the lead man finishes asking his men, a scream of pained terror rends the air. It's a sound that's so tortured, so broken, it will haunt me until the day I die.

I scramble to follow as the men and woman sprint toward the wall of the ruins on the other side of the camp, but Emma grabs my arm and squeezes tight. Her nails puncture my skin. For a millisecond, I want to tear myself away, but one look at her tearstained face and I know she's reliving the same hell Annalise must be going through in her mind.

Instead, I pull her hand from my arm, grasping it tightly in my own, and head toward the shouting. The woman drags Annalise from behind the wall and shoves her toward us. Annalise, head bowed, stumbles as she struggles to hold her shirt over her chest and runs on unsteady legs toward me.

It's been hours since we've been taken to the bathroom, and longer still since we were given any food or water. Dehydration is a serious concern. It's a wonder that my body can produce any tears at all. I cry as I rock Annalise in my arms, but I know now that any comfort I offer is a thing of the past.

We've been tied hand and foot. It's as if the man pulling Roberts's strings thinks Annalise was to blame for those assholes assaulting her, or they don't trust Roberts and his men to guard us. For now, it's a barrier to any escape we planned. Personally, I think they're afraid I'm going to kill them in their sleep. I would if I could, but I'm getting worse. Probably an infection. Lack of food isn't helping, not that I'm hungry. The small amount of water we were given when we got here wasn't enough to clean our faces properly, let alone cleanse away the rest of his blood to see if I have any other wounds. Does it really matter?

The thought of never seeing Truex again leaves a huge hole right in the center of me. I can feel my will to live seeping out of me as easily as my tears.

The only thing that gives me the strength to hang on instead of drifting away is Emma and Annalise. Her conviction that Raven will come for us is both crazy and awe inspiring. To have that much faith after what that girl has been through? I'll fight until she doesn't need me, or until I cannot physically do it anymore.

Eyes closed, I concentrate on reviving the connection to Truex or Tarrik through our bond, but either he's gone or I'm too weak to reach him. I'll let the girls rest a bit longer and then we'll get to work on these ropes. If we die trying to get away it will be better than whatever these asshole kidnappers have planned for us.

"Well, I would guess me finding you here is about to fuck up your day." At the sound of Raven's voice, muscles that I didn't even realize were taut clench tighter and then relax.

At first, I think she's talking to me, but instead, her attention is on the man kneeling next to us in the confined space. How did I not realize he was here? Right next to us? He could have killed us all or stolen Annalise away again, and this time, she's unable to fight back.

Annalise awakens. Her soft sobs of terror are heart-wrenching. She jolts away from the man, banging against me. My vision flashes white as pain stabs through me, stealing the air from my lungs and the cry of agonizing pain from my lips. Black spots dance before me as I struggle to stay conscious.

When I'm finally able to focus, I catch a hint of surprise in the man's eyes, though it quickly changes to a twinkle of mischief.

"Not just mine, little queen." The rogue smiles.

There's a burst of movement as a man grabs Raven from behind. She doesn't panic or falter. In fact, she slumps in the man's arms before clamping a fist onto his crotch.

The whine of pain he makes and the angry determination on Raven's face tells me this is a game of chicken, a contest of wills, and by God, the man drops to his knees, cradling his junk and rocking like a baby on the floor.

That's when I notice the man next to us is reaching out to touch Annalise, offering her soft sounds of reassurance as she tries to worm and jostle her way behind me, without much luck. Her struggles are ineffectual as she gasps, sobs, and practically hyperventilates in her quest to get away.

The side of the tents is torn open, allowing in more light. The jagged ripping noise is loud over Annalise's small whimpers. The prince, large and angry, steps through the hole he's created. First, he looks Raven over and then turns to check on us.

"Release them," he growls. The man raises his eyebrows but does as Prince Orion says. He pulls a knife from his boot and cuts away our bindings. Just as he gently releases the last rope holding Annalise's hands, a scream and then gunshots echo in the distance.

"Get down!" Raven hisses.

I can't help the cry of pain that leaves my lips as the prince lands on top of me and Annalise, protecting us with his body. I'm hardly aware of the bullets turning the tent into Swiss cheese, as more pain washes over me and I fight not to puke again.

Suddenly, the prince is up, ripping through the tattered remnants of the tent. I'm so exhausted and weak, I struggle to raise myself up off the ground. I lay there staring at the sky, unable to move. Would a bullet be a lesser evil than just giving up?

Lightning flashes through the clear sky above me, close enough that my sweaty braids move from the colossal force of it as it slams to the ground nearby. Screams fill the air. How we are not all dead, I do not know.

A tingle of magic skates over my skin, and for a moment, I'm back in Truex's arms, resting against his warm, strong body, and the pain I'm feeling stills. I allow myself to drift along to the beautiful and musical notes of love, remembering and reliving our last moments of happiness together.

Seconds, minutes, or maybe hours later, someone pulls at me, calling my name. But I'm too lost to answer. Strong arms lift me, but they're not the ones I long for. A discordant note, flat and out of tune, echoes, banging against my consciousness. A bit of wrongness, bringing me back to awareness and pain, physical and emotional. This man smells different. Not bad, just not Truex. I'm relieved when he lays me back on the ground, because his arms are not the ones I want wrapped around me.

"Nola? I have water. Can you drink it?" I feel wetness on my lips, and even though it's almost hot, it tastes sweet as it dribbles over the parched surface of my tongue. "Not too much at first, okay?" Raven asks as she begins to bathe my face.

"Her arm is broken," Annalise whispers. "She was throwing up too."

Strong fingers work their way under my hair, and I cringe when they press against the sore spot on the back of my head.

"She probably has a concussion. Let me see what I can do to make her more comfortable."

"Don't bother." My words are barely more than a croak as I force them past the grief restricting my throat. "It... I don't want to without...Truex." Tears leak, running into the braids where my temples meet my ears.

"Honey, listen to me. Truex is alive. He was hurt, but he has a good chance of pulling through. You need to let us help you so you can go to him. Do you understand?"

I open my eyes to see Raven kneeling over me, looking down at me with concern written across her dirty but still lovely face.

"He's alive? But I saw him die, Raven. I felt it." No, this must be a wicked lie, a terrible nightmare. I shake my head in denial, groaning at the pain and dizziness it causes. Dare I believe her? Her voice holds no deception, and though I don't know her well, we have become friends of sorts. Raven's eyes convey honesty. She believes what she says.

"He was alive when we left to come get you. He wasn't conscious, but he was breathing. Tarrik, Beach, and, if I were to guess, even your friend Jasmine are watching over him until I can get you back to take care of him."

"Really? Please...don't lie. He's truly alive? But how?"

"Drink some more water and let me heal you. Then I'll tell you all I know, okay?"

"Blackmail?"

Her lips quirk. "Whatever works."

"But...you're certain? Truex..."

"Yes, now let me help you so we can both go see this fabled Summer's Veil."

"Okay."

"Are you okay, Emma?" Raven switches her attention from me to my friend as Zekiel helps her over to us.

I glance beyond Raven to see most of our kidnappers have been tied up by some of the warriors. If it were up to me, I would kill them all for what they've put us through. Roberts stands hunched between two warriors, waiting his turn, but I notice his chin lifts and his eyes turn hard when he hears Emma's name.

"I've been cramping," Emma whispers.

"You need to lie down and get your feet up. It's not good for the baby. You're probably dehydrated too. We'll have some water for you soon." Raven reaches out to steady her as Zekiel helps her lie next to me.

"You goddamned whore!" William Roberts screams as he throws his body backward and then forward, breaking free from those holding him. He storms toward us.

Emma cringes, folding in on herself while gripping her stomach. It isn't Orion or even Zekiel who stops him. It's a dark-haired man I didn't even realize was standing near us until he moves faster than lightning to intercept Roberts. How I missed seeing him and the men standing with him is a mystery, because this man has presence. His bone structure is beautiful, and his hair looks as if he's just stepped out of a salon. He's wearing fitted black pants and a pristine billowing white shirt. He looks like a movie-star pirate. They all do. I'll have to tell Jasmine and the girls there are pirates in this new realm. It gives new meaning to the phrase booty call, for sure.

He grabs the charging man as Roberts curses, throwing disgusting slurs at Emma. The pirate tosses him across the clearing, away from us. The other similarly dressed men follow, beating Roberts. Lightning flashes in my periphery.

Roberts screams just like he did in my vision, and I know he's finally met his demise.

I can't sit up to see what's going on, but I hear the pirate captain bark orders at someone to dispose of the body. Then he's there, pushing Zekiel aside, before dropping to his knees beside Emma. I stare in wonder at the spectacular ebony wings flaring out behind him. His face is severe, and an honest-to-God fang flashes when he snarls. If Truex look otherworldly, this dude looks like a fallen angel mixed with a swashbuckling pirate.

Emma trembles beside me. She gasps as he touches her, his eyes glowing with rage. Oh, my.

"She needs calm right now, Caspian," Raven says softly but firmly.

Wait a minute, she knows him? He looks like he wants to rip Raven's head off for interrupting him, but instead, he gives one sharp nod. He says something to Emma too low for me to hear before rising and storming away.

* * *

It's two days before I can travel, if not comfortably, then at least without puking all over the place. We've been afraid to move Emma too, until this morning. We're riding back to our camp in the truck bed again, not because it's too stuffy in the cab, but because Annalise is having trouble being close to any of the men.

She's sitting between Raven and me with her head on Raven's shoulder, holding both of our hands in hers as she dozes. She refuses to talk about what happened. Part of me doesn't blame her, I'm having a hard time vocalizing how I feel about what happened to us too.

"How're you holding up?" Emma whispers from my other side.

"I'm okay. Well, I'll be okay when I see Truex again." *If I see Truex again.* I still can't feel him through our link. It's just gone. Not there. Radio silence.

We ride in silence for a few minutes, my thoughts taking me back down that dark path that I'm ashamed to admit I was ready to run down, without much thought to anyone else. I owe Annalise and Emma so much.

"How about you? Any more cramps?"

"Not since last night. I do have to pee, but I can hold it for a while longer. Annalise just fell asleep, and I hate to wake her. She's not doing well."

"No. She's not. None of us are, are we?"

We lapse into silence, watching the dry, barren landscape disappear over the tailgate until we both fall asleep.

I wake sometime later to stillness and Emma's groan.

"Oh God, are you okay? Is it the baby?" I'm about to raise the alarm when Emma snorts.

"No, it's not the baby, but now I *really* have to pee. You're lucky we're not sitting in a puddle right now."

She groans again as she moves. "I have to go so bad, I'm afraid to move! How am I going to stand up?"

I can't help it, despite all the worry and uncertainty, I snicker loud enough to rouse both Annalise and Raven. *Huh, Raven actually sleeps. I was beginning to think she might be that woman with the golden truth-telling lasso in disguise.*

"Emma has to pee but can't move, or she'll create the great flood." I announce.

Raven grins but Annalise barely smiles.

"Orion?" Raven looks around for her mate, waving him over as he and the other men set up our camp for the night.

It's really kind of sweet how these guys bend over backward to do everything for this fiercely independent woman.

"Emma has to use the facilities," Raven says when he reaches us, unaware of the trigger she's just pulled. Annalise flinches, no doubt remembering how this whole fiasco of being kidnapped started.

Pain sharp and pure lances my heart. I'm not the only one affected by Raven's innocent statement. Annalise briefly meets my gaze, shame dropping over her features like a heavy blanket. I squeeze her hand, letting her know that I'm here for her. Letting her know I understand even when the pain steals my breath. It's at that moment I feel something effervesce deep inside me almost like an internal tickle fizzing and popping, there and then gone, and suddenly back again strong and vibrating.

I gasp as tears start rolling down my face. Annalise tugs at my hand. I turn my head, meeting her gaze.

"He's alive," I whisper.

Chapter 9

Nola

Two days later, we catch up with the rest of our group just as they reach the foothills of Summer's Veil. I'm practically bouncing in place waiting for the truck to stop, not because of the rough path we've taken, but because I can't wait to see Truex. I can feel him, present and steady through our link, but I'll feel so much better when I can see him with my own two eyes. To see that he's going to be okay.

Finally! The truck stops. I twist as far as I can, looking over the side of the truck for him. My heart pauses and then picks up a galloping rhythm as I see Truex and Tarrik shoulder to shoulder, pushing through the crowd, coming toward me.

I can't take my eyes off him as I catalog every change, every nuance. He's thinner. His natural grace is a little stilted. Truex's once-golden skin is now pale and sallow. His cheeks are hollowed out. He hasn't healed completely, but we can do that together.

I can't stop the cheek aching smile that stretches across my face as he stops at the side of the truck. His eyes track over my face and body in the same manner that mine do his. I pull my hand from Annalise and struggle onto my knees and then my feet. Truex raises his arms, but Tarrik pushes him aside and takes over the duty of lifting me down from the bed of the truck. Truex frowns but allows his brothers help.

"Nola." He pulls me into his arms, careful of my wrist. I lean against him, careful of his chest, and raise my lips to meet his. Both of us pour everything we feel into it.

"Truex," I whisper against his lips before he kisses me with growing passion.

"Enough of that. Neither of you is in any condition to handle where you think this is going," Raven interrupts. "Besides, the birth control brigade will be here any second. They do not need this kind of education right now."

I giggle, remembering our campfire and coffee conversation. Was it only a few days ago? It seems like a lifetime, and in some ways, it was.

Orion gently lifts first Emma and then Annalise down from the truck bed. Annalise, head bowed, pushes in next to me. Truex gives me a questioning look, but I shake my head, silently telling him *not now*.

"I'm sorry," Annalise whispers with a quick glance at Truex and Tarrik. "It's my fault you were hurt. That Nola and Emma were hurt. That we were taken."

I want to offer a denial, but Zekiel comes forward and offers his arm to Emma. She frowns but takes it as Annalise shrinks away from him.

"My lady Annalise, may I escort you to your new home?" Tarrik offers Annalise his arm, his manner gentle and patient. "There is a room available right next to Truex and Nola's room, with mine just beyond if you need anything."

"T-thank you," she whispers.

"You will love Summer's Veil. It is its own entity. Whatever you desire, within reason of course, Summer's Veil will provide it for you. It will also protect you." He tucks her hand in the crook of his arm. "You are safe here, and of course, you may call on me if you have need."

She nods, her face pinkening when she notices we're paying attention to them.

Just then, we're swarmed by all of Raven's children, chattering and welcoming us back into the fold. I want to hug Tarrik for being so perceptive. Truex offers me his arm, patting my hand in understanding.

Jasmine, Tanni, and Ginger follow behind the kids waiting their turn to welcome us. I hug Jasmine, happy to see my friend.

"Well then, now that we are all accounted for, let us welcome our new family to Summer's Veil." Orion leads the way through the group of children and up through the adults gathered. We pass through a tall stand of pines and walk into a pristine meadow.

"Oh. My. God!" Raven's awe-filled whisper is echoed by the other humans as we finally step into the clearing. "It looks like Stonehenge."

I stand and stare, mouth hanging open. "It looks like something out of a fairy tale," I breathe. And indeed, it does. The stone monoliths are blanketed in snow so white and sparkly, they almost glow against the backdrop of green pines and majestic mountains touching the crisp cerulean sky. It's breathtakingly beautiful. My attention is pulled away by the voice of Prince Orion.

"Behold, Lady Raven, Queen of Summer's Veil. Queen of Elfame," he announces with confidence and ceremony. "Queen of my heart."

I gasp in surprise and then cheer for my friend as she kisses her prince. He swings her into his arms and steps through a glowing blue gap between the stones that will take us beneath the mountain and into the haven of Truex's home.

We follow much more sedately behind them. The wonder of Summer's Veil is like nothing I can describe. I have nothing to compare it to. Summer's Veil is a world in and of itself. It has its own sun, moon, and stars, as well as miles of fields, hills, forests, and streams. I can't wait to explore when I'm rested.

Annalise and Emma decide they'd be more comfortable sharing a room. I think it's a good idea. Neither of them should be alone after all they've gone through. After we finally get them settled, I'm exhausted, and I can tell Truex is dragging too.

"You know what I need?" I ask Truex.

"Tell me, and it is yours." No equivocation—he just offers up everything to me.

"I need a hot bath and a nap with you beside me."

"Done."

Truex

I lie here next to Nola, watching the soft play of fairy lights highlighting her hair and softening the bruises still visible across her face. I marvel at her strength, her beauty, her compassion for others. Gently, I reach out a finger to touch her splinted wrist. Sadness wells within me that I am the cause of so many of her injuries.

She stirs, stretching as her eyelids flutter open. "Truex?"

I swallow, suddenly overcome. The way she says my name and the softness in her deep brown eyes give me hope that she might be feeling the same way as I am. We are destined mates, but that doesn't mean she has to have feelings for me.

It has happened in the past that mates disregarded the importance of linking by kismet, but they were not love matches, which eventually led to discord and madness.

"What is it?" Concern furrows her brow.

"I..."

"Just tell me." She stiffens and pulls away. It's not a physical movement, but an emotional one. I am making a mess of this.

"I love you." There. I put it out there.

"You... I... What?"

"I love you." It's freeing to say it. I say it again, smiling like a fool. "I. Love. You."

"You love me?" The soft confusion on her face is endearing.

"I do."

"Are you certain?"

"I am."

"No one has ever said that to me before."

"I am not just saying it. I am feeling it, sharing it, and from now until the ever after, I am living it. I will tell you and show you every single day for the rest of our lives. I will cherish only you, breathe only you, love only you."

I wait for her response. Minutes pass, but I don't push. Our connection is solid, and I can see she is in her head, having an internal conversation. Who knew three simple little words would throw my lady off her stride? But Nola is complicated. She's been through the fire more than once and come out the other side intact. I would wait for her forever if need be.

Nola finally blinks, coming back from wherever she has been. A smile sweeter than honey forms on her lips as she finally gives me the words.

"I love you too, Truex."

I lean in and gently place a soft kiss on her luscious mouth. Nola moans, squirming to be closer to me, touching the seam of my lips with her tongue, asking for more, but I pull away.

"Hold on, woman. You are in no condition to take this further."

"Oh, and you think you are? You were shot. You almost d-died."

Rather than argue with her, I agree. "I did. I was shot with your human weapons. Unfortunately, it seems the Fae are allergic to lead magic but our queen is well versed in healing and saved me. I could stand to convalesce for a couple more days with you here beside me." I run a finger over her cheek, catching the tear that has escaped. "We will have a lifetime to be intimate after we are both sufficiently healed."

"I love how that sounds, and I love you," she whispers, emotion making her voice waver.

"I love you most, woman."

Epilogue

Caspian

"I'm all right," the upstart human queen of the Fae tells her mate. "What was the explosion? And where did it come from? Jahzuah? Will you check on James, please?"

"No need, lady queen. Your sniper is here." I, along with my men, push the human sniper into view, sneering at those who startle. I'm disappointed with those who don't. I do love making a grand entrance, after all.

"Late to the party as usual, aren't you, Caspian?" Severill, the Infernion leader taunts me.

Gods, I hate him. If there's one being in all the realms more arrogant than I, it would be Severill.

"James? It's good to see you. I need the first aid bag from the truck. Hell, we need the whole truck, and the water too." The feisty little human queen ignores me completely. I'll admit, I don't like it. I want her to notice me, but all she sees is her mate. She would have made a good addition to our breeding agenda, providing strong warriors sons and fertile daughters.

"Arden, go with him," the Fae prince orders as he places himself at his mate's back.

The human, James, reclaims his weapon from the hands of my warrior Raziel. We relieved him of it when we arrived at the skirmish between the Fae and the traffickers.

"I am interested to learn more about these weapons you humans use." I don't ask the human or use his name the queen has called him, I tell him.

The human world has held a fascination for our kind for centuries. The new and modern accomplishments of the last two hundred years especially.

"Talk to my lady," the sniper quips before hurrying away.

Cocky bastard.

"Okay, people. We need to see to Nola and the girls," the Lady Raven directs the Fae. "Someone needs to see if we can salvage any of the material from that tent and create a blind for some shade. Orion, can you move her?" The human queen assesses the site. "Over there."

She is magnificent.

"We need to gather wood for a pyre. There is no way we will be able to dig a big enough grave in this dry, packed ground for the dead." Prince Orion glances at me.

Does he expect me to help them beyond me saving their asses?

It's then that I notice one of his men helping a lovely but distressed woman over to the queen. A viciousness I've never felt before rises in me. I want to rip his arms off for touching her. If she touched him back with any sort of affection, I would.

"Are you okay, Emma?" the queen asks.

The girl's expression from what I can see, is pain filled and stressed.

She whispers something I don't catch as the Fae warrior helps her lay beside the other injured woman.

"Get your feet up. It's not good for the baby. You're probably dehydrated, too. We'll have some water for you soon," the queen reassures her.

Wait. A baby?

"You goddamned cheating slut!" A human man struggles against the arms restraining him, crazy eyes locked on the woman. "You're going to burn in hell! See if you don't! I'ma send you there myself, you filthy monster's whore!" Spittle flies from the man's mouth as he spews his filth. He breaks free of those holding him, storming toward the women.

Emma, cringes, folding in on herself while gripping her stomach. There is no doubt where the bruises on her have come from.

Rages floods my mind; a seething pool of chaos where normally cold decisiveness prevails. There is no way he'll ever touch her again. No male of any race will.

I grab the man, stopping him from reaching her. His vile words continue as he presses toward the girl. Vengeance, pure and unadulterated, boils within me. I pound my fists into him over and over before tossing him across the clearing away from her. My warriors follow, doling out punishment to the animal that would have beaten a defenseless woman in front of us all.

When I think he's had enough, I send a bolt of lightning whipping through his body, frying him where he lies.

"Dispose of that filth!" I snarl to my men as I turn and head back to the girl. Her name is Emma, I remind myself. I shove Orion's warrior out of the way and drop to my knees beside her.

She trembles, I'm not sure at that moment if it's because of pain, fear of her abuser, or fear of me, but her reaction stings my ego and squeezes my heart. I stare into her eyes and feel the first silken string of connection bind us.

I catalog everything about her. The dirty red-gold hair, the misty pain filled hazel of her eyes, the dark bruises obliterating the sprinkle of gingered freckles across her cheekbones, the split in her soft pink lip, the way she's shakes with stress and fear.

Her eyes flare for a second, a recognition if you will, but then she looks away, the skin that's not bruised flushing pink and then paling with shame. Fury boils within me. I squeeze my hands into fists, fighting the urge to summon lightning.

"She needs calm right now, Caspian," Raven admonishes.

I glare at the queen of two races, feeling volatile in my rage, impotent in my ability to steal Emma away when she needs this little queen's care.

I force myself to my feet. Without a word, I turn, calling my wings and magic to the fore. I throw myself into the sky, away from the woman damaged by another man's hands. I leave her lying in the dirt. A woman pregnant with another man's child. Life truly is a wicked bitch. I'll be back after she heals and has that baby. I vow it. The thought of sharing her with anyone including the sentinels is reprehensible. No one, not the prince, his new queen, Severill, or Emma herself will stand in my way because she is mine. She is the woman that destiny has chosen to be my mate. It's only a matter of time before I claim her.

About Jaelle Keyes

SUGAR IN A DARK WORLD~

I write the romance stories I love to read. Contemporary, Paranormal, alternate realities? MF, MFM, misfit witches, motorcycle clubs, shifters, angels, demons, humor, spice, and action? Anything goes as long as there's an HEA/HFN!

In reality, I'm just a quirky girl with an enormous love for reading sultry, slow burn, romance stories. Give me a cup of coffee or tea, a crunchy sweet, a good love story, and maybe a fuzzy pup or two to snuggle, and I've found my happy place. Sound familiar? Then we should be friends!

Please consider joining my reader's group- **Bean Stalkers & Book Reapers** and my author page **Jaelle Keyes** on Facebook and you can find all my social media links here: https://linktr.ee/JaelleKeyesAuthor

My books are available on several platforms. You can find my books, discover the signing events I'll be attending, and stay current with new releases by subscribing to my newsletter when you sign up to receive this complimentary story– SNOW WITCHES ALLOWED here: https://www.jaellekeyes.com

I appreciate you.

Happy reading,

Other Titles By Jaelle Keyes

Witch I Wish You Would Series
Destiny's A Witch- https://books2read.com/u/brBRpk
Life's A Witch- https://books2read.com/u/38YWWZ

The Fallen MC Midwest Series
Spelled In Wonder- https://books2read.com/u/38Y0EV
Spelled In Magic-https://books2read.com/u/3GpqnP
Spelled In Lies- https://books2read.com/u/3RP56D

The Merciless Few MC Series
Tinsel & Chrome: The Merciless Few MC Charity Anthology- https://www.amazon.com/Tinsel-Chrome-Merciless-Charity-Anthology-ebook/dp/B0DB65MBXZ